CITADEL: CHILDREN OF LIGHT

CITADEL: CHILDREN OF LIGHT

BOOK THREE OF CITADEL

J. KEVIN TUMLINSON

KNOVELTON

For you, Faithful Reader.
Cheesy as it sounds — still true.
Thanks for sticking around

CHAPTER 1

THE CHAIRMAN NEVER SHOUTED IF HE COULD HELP IT. Uttering something in a calm and civil tone made it sound all the more threatening.

"You utter imbecile," the Chairman said in a low and rumbling register.

The lackey before him was a mid-level manager, and a mid-level member of Earth First. The Chairman hadn't bothered learning his name. It might not be needed much longer.

The man cringed. "Sir, I apologize. We were tracking the vessel when it simply ... *vanished*." He said this last part with a shrug meant as some sort of absolution.

"It never arrived at Taggart's moon?" the Chairman asked, quietly.

"No, sir," the man said.

"There was no detonation?"

A pause. "No, sir. We would have detected something from the sensor arrays in the lightrail hubs. There wasn't so much as a blip. The vessel checked in at one of the hubs a couple of months ago, and then it was gone. It should have arrived at the moon by now, but there's been no sign of it. I have hundreds of operatives combing data to discover what could have happened. Another vessel left that hub a few days ago and has reported nothing by relay. Our investigation is hampered, sir, by the delay of having to send probes to the hubs."

"I am familiar with the limitations of communication over light years."

The Chairman opened a small wooden box on his desk. This was real wood, from the days of wild tree growth, not the artificially bred and grown trees from one of the arbor museums. It was an antique, handed down from one Chairman to the next in an unbroken line. It had held everything from cigars to human fingers, in its time — some of the former Chairmen were not as cultivated as he. For his turn with the box, he had chosen to fill it with butterscotch candies in bright yellow wrappers.

He took one of these and slowly unwrapped it, then popped it in his mouth. It was the only sweet he allowed himself. It was delicious.

"You have 24 hours to find that vessel, or to otherwise confirm that both Taggart and Corey have perished." The ice in the Chairman's voice would mean many sleepless nights for the middle manager. What few remained.

"Yes, sir," the middle manager said. He turned and left the Chairman's office without another word and with no need for dismissal.

The Chairman sucked on the hard candy and thought about Taggart and Corey. Mostly he thought about Taggart. Corey was a nuisance, a blister on the heel. His absence had not gone unnoticed, of course. The media had picked up the story of the poster child of Earth First boarding a colony vessel, and for months there had been cheeky stories and jibes directed at the organization.

The Chairman had ordered that all of this be ignored. No comment, no reaction. In decades past he had found that the best approach to bad press was to wait and let it run its course. In time it would fade, because in time no one would remember who Corey was.

Vid stars? Please. They had no lasting impact on the world. They were pretty faces who could temporarily hold the attention of an audience riddled with ADHD. Given time, everything about this story would fade from memory, replaced by rumors of another celebrity having sex with a dolphin or something.

Taggart was the real problem for Earth First.

His plan was interesting, the Chairman was forced to admit. Taking control of the lightrail network would mean owning all of the colonies, and having the power to evict the alien shrubs for good. These ridiculous peace treaties and cultural exchanges could stop, then. The Esool would be at the mercy of Taggart.

But Taggart was not a purist. He was a legacy in Earth First, but also something of an enigma. His ancestors, over a hundred years ago, had picked up the pieces after the destruction of the First Colony vessel, coming to power (and not a small amount of wealth) by taking on the technology developed by John Thomas Paris and his team, developing it into the first generation of colony vessels. It was because of the Taggart family that humans were able to leave Earth.

And yet, the Taggarts were among the founding members of Earth First — an organization with the clearly stated goal of *preventing* colonization. For almost two centuries the Taggart family had walked the line between enabling colonization and rallying for its destruction. The previous Chairmen, indeed all previous generations of Earth First leaders and members, had questioned the Taggart commitment and resolve over the years. But the *money* ...

It always came back to the money. In perhaps the greatest of ironies, the organization that nearly killed the colony program at its birth was built on money *made* from colonization.

The Taggarts were the largest financial contributors for Earth First, and always had been. Without their funding, the organization simply would never have existed. It was their initial funding that earned the Taggarts a place in the leadership of Earth First. A Taggart had always been at the helm.

There had long been a suspicion, in the upper echelons of Earth First, that the Taggarts had funded the organization and the sabotage of First Colony as a means of hostile takeover, to seize all of the patents and technology that the Paris team had exclusive access to.

The prevailing sentiment that the Earth was overcrowded, that the only hope was to spread humanity among the stars, had helped to draw millions to the side of colonization. Taggart Industries made billions from accommodating that movement.

For those who saw colonization as an *end* to civilization, Taggart industries made equally as much profit by supplying stasis technology to keep the wealthiest alive for long stretches of history. They also supplied equipment used in industry and manufacturing, household appliances, recreational technology, and pre-fab housing for lower income areas. Taggart — the *current* Taggart — was rich and powerful specifically because everyone was his customer.

The Chairman admired this, though he'd never admit it. The few times he'd met Taggart, the man seemed genuinely brilliant, as had his father and grandfather. There was something impressive about brilliance of that sort, though it made Taggart a notoriously difficult man to control.

Now Taggart had meticulously designed a hostile takeover of the lightrail —the very system his family had helped to build, the nervous system of the colonies. Left undisturbed, Taggart would have likely become an emperor.

But for now he was simply *missing*.

Missing was a good start, but confirmed dead was preferable.

The Chairman touched the surface of his desk and there was a chirp to indicate an open comm. "Rudford," the Chairman said quietly.

"Yes, sir," Rudford said, equally as quiet.

"I want every bit of data that exists regarding Taggart's moon."

"You'll have it within the hour," Rudford said before disconnecting.

The Chairman liked Rudford. He was a frightening man of the sort that used to dominate history. In another time, Rudford might have been a Napoleon, or perhaps an Attila. He could lead by ruthlessness, if he chose. Which was why the Chairman had chosen *him*, and had a small explosive device implanted in the man's brain. His sociopathic tendencies could be useful, but it wouldn't do to allow him to roam unchecked. Still, for all of that, Rudford did not seem to mind his enforced servitude. He thrived in it, actually. He took enormous pleasure in being second in command. Someday he might make a wonderful Chairman.

Until then, Rudford would serve, and within an hour the Chairman would have all the information he needed to start finding leverage within Taggart's own organization. He would own Taggart's moon, soon enough.

He would own the means to shut down the lightrail forever.

ALAN WAS FRUSTRATED with the results.

Moments before, the man on the exam table had been in the thrall of the Current — a living creature that appeared to be made of pure energy. That was amazing. It was incredible. And at the moment, it seemed to be over.

The patterns had all changed. There was suddenly no sign of the Current's influence at all. The man was now just *himself* — one more wealthy colonist stranded on this world.

Stranded by me. He shook his head, trying to stay focused on the work instead of the mistakes.

It was bad enough that the Current seem to have vanished. Adding to the frustration, for Alan, was the fact that the secondary waveform — the one implanted in the man while he slept in stasis— was also gone. Alan had put that waveform there, and for weeks now he had worked day and night, under guard and in captivity, to discover a way to reverse the damage he'd done. This was the first sign that it was possible, and Alan had no idea how it happened.

The former host had no memory of what had happened over the past few days or weeks. He was dazed, a little dehydrated, and kept referring to the "strange dream" he'd been having. He wasn't clear on details, and nothing he said was of much help to Alan.

It was clear that the Current was no longer present in either the host or in the room. Alan's working theory, at the moment, was that the Current had somehow absorbed the foreign waveform before leaving the man behind.

That was exciting news, because if that was true, the

Current could be the key to returning all of the colonists to normal. It was also frightening, because, removing the waveforms would effectively kill all of the First Colony personalities.

That was the greatest irony. Alan started all of this, set this series of events into motion, specifically to *restore* those personalities and redeem the man accused of killing them all.

John Thomas Paris — the man known to history as "the murderer of worlds," among other less flattering titles — had been a close friend to Alan's father. In fact, Alan's real name was John Thomas Alan, named in honor of his father's best friend.

Alan had successfully executed a plan that took over a hundred years to complete, overcoming the uncertainty of a century of advancement and cultural evolution to achieve his goal. And it had worked. His father, Louis Alan, now lived again, in the body of a man named Taggart.

But he could never have predicted this twist. To fix the chaos and destruction he had caused, he would commit the very crime for which Uncle John — *Thomas*, Alan reminded himself — had been accused.

Thomas saw his friends and colleagues murdered in a terrorist attack, and was then wrongfully imprisoned, sentenced to death for the crime. He had survived in stasis over the past century because of Alan's plan. Now he would see his friends die all over again.

What sort of monster had Alan become? What would his father think?

Alan looked around the lab. There were others in the room. Guards, mostly. Two of the guards were constant companions these days. Somar, the Esool captain, had ordered that Alan remain under constant watch. Alan accepted that. In the end, Somar had shown Alan a tremendous mercy by letting him live, and by letting his father work alongside him. True, his father currently resided in the body of Taggart ...

Alan froze. His father. In Taggart's body.

He'd left the lab nearly half an hour ago, acting a bit strange. Maybe a little dazed.

Alan turned sharply toward the door, taking an involuntary step toward it. The guards, alert to his sudden movements, drew their weapons and ordered him to stand back, to put his hands up.

Alan was just about to explain — about his father, about Taggart, about his sudden new theory — when there was a tremendous explosion somewhere in the colony. The lab shook, and people stumbled and fell from the shockwave of it. Alan managed to keep himself upright by holding on to the edge of the examining table, where the former host was wailing and covering his head with his hands.

Whatever that was, it was big, Alan thought. With a sudden dread, he realized that there was only one thing in the budding new colony that would have enough stored energy to cause an explosion of that size.

"We have to get to the Citadel tower!" he shouted, and ran for the door of the lab. The guards regained their footing and came after him, weapons drawn. Alan wasn't sure if they were going *with* him to investigate, or trying to *arrest* him for fleeing. They could be taking aim, about to fire molecular disruption disks into his back, putting him out of the colony's misery once and for all.

He'd know soon enough.

MITCH WOKE **in a fit of coughing**. A thick cloud of dust and smoke obscured everything — for a disorienting moment his addled brain thought he was coming out of stasis. He coughed again, felt the ragged and burning pain in his lungs, and reality came rushing back.

The wedding.

Reilly!

He rolled onto his side and saw her there, laying on the ground, partially covered in debris, smoke curling in tendrils over her.

His heart pounded as he crawled toward her, fear chilling him and constricting his lungs even more than the smoke was doing, making it even harder for him to breath. It couldn't be this way. Not after everything. Not after surviving on that platform, after surviving the crash on this world. To lose her here, now, in this way ...

She groaned and coughed, and Mitch felt himself come to life. He suddenly had the energy to get to his feet, to reach for the debris covering her and hoist it away. In moments he had her in his arms, and was struggling to get her away from the smoke and dust. It was hard to see. Smoke mingled with tears in his eyes.

She groaned again as Mitch set her safely on the ground, near a copse of trees acting as a filter to all the smoke. He checked her pulse, which felt strong, and tried to wake her. "Reilly? Reilly are you ok? Baby, can you hear me?" Again she groaned. He checked her for injuries and found deep bruising on her left side and arm. There was a knot forming on her forehead. She'd taken a pretty serious hit. Mitch, worried, knew he had to find a doctor. Looking back through the swirling mess of smoke and drifting ash at the base of the Citadel tower, he realized that a lot of people would need help.

His instinct was to rush toward the wreckage, to take charge, to organize a rescue effort. For the first time in his life, however, his emotions overwhelmed his instinct. He couldn't leave her. He *couldn't*. He had to stay. He had to ... he had to ...

"Help," someone said weakly.

Mitch looked to see Janet struggling to her feet. He only hesitated a second, looking at Reilly once more, making sure she was breathing, that she was fine. He got to his feet and rushed to Janet's side.

She was a little scraped up, but seemed ok. He helped her stand, guiding her to where Reilly lay beneath the trees. As he did, he spotted Thomas laying on his back among the rubble. He was unconscious, but Mitch caught sight of his chest rising and falling. That was good. Thomas would be ok. Thomas was the *king* of ok.

Mitch started to move again but stopped in his tracks, his hand on Janet's arm.

"Oh my God," Janet said, seeing what had caught Mitch's attention.

Somar, the Esool captain, had been thrown backwards by the blast. He was sprawled on a pile of debris. A large shaft of jagged metal was jutting through his chest.

Mitch glanced at Janet, who was already pulling away. "Go," she said.

He gestured toward Thomas. "Someone needs to get him out of there," he said. "Are you steady enough to get some help, organize a response team?"

She nodded, and Mitch ran to Somar's side.

Somar moved slightly as Mitch approached. "Captain," Mitch said, kneeling beside him.

"Mister ... Garrison," Somar said, then sputtered and coughed.

"Captain, don't try to talk. Don't move. I have to get some help. You're badly injured."

"It is quite serious," Somar said. "But I can seal the wound." He sounded weak, but determined. Mitch leaned back and watched as the wound did seem to seal around the debris. "Mister Garrison, if you will be so kind as to remove the debris, I ..." he coughed a few times, wincing. "I have stopped the bleeding."

Mitch was dubious, but didn't want to argue. He had heard the rumors of the Captain being able to heal himself, after Jack and his crew attacked him. He'd also heard the stories about the Esool — that they could heal their wounded in battle. There were stories of humans fighting their way onto Esool ships, leaving the wounded enemy in their wake as they made their way to the bridge of the vessel, only to find themselves surrounded in a corridor they thought they had cleared.

That was before. That was the enemy. This was Somar. His friend. His Captain.

Mitch gripped the shard of metal, and counting to three for Somar's benefit, he yanked hard and pulled the metal free.

Somar gasped and cried out, and the blood immediately began to flow in green rivulets from the wound, down Somar's side. Mitch instantly regretted removing the shard. He took off his shirt and waded it into a ball, pushing it onto Somar's chest to help staunch the bleeding.

"I ... fear the damage was worse than my first assessment," Somar said weakly.

"I think you could be right," Mitch said, trying to smile. It was forced, and he wasn't sure it inspired any confidence. "Captain, is there anything I can do? I heard about the events by the river. Do I need to get you to water?"

Somar shook his head. "I'm afraid ... " he winced, "... the injury may be too grave ... for that to be effective," he said, struggling.

"What can I do? How can I help?"

Somar smiled. "You can tend to others, Mister Garrison. Ensure that as many survive ... as possible," and with that the Captain closed his eyes.

Mitch felt an instant of panic, and reached to feel Somar's pulse.

Did the Esool even have pulses? Did they have carotid arteries? Would it be in the same place?

To his relief, Mitch felt a thready pulse in the alien's neck, close to where Mitch had expected it to be.

Passed out, Mitch thought. *Just passed out. Good.*

But worse things could be on their way if Somar didn't receive immediate medical attention. Mitch looked up to see Janet and some others carrying Thomas and another survivor out to the tree line. "Janet!" Mitch cried. "Find Doctor Michaels, fast!"

Janet turned, and was holding her side as she took in what Mitch was saying. She nodded and ran in search of the doctor.

Mitch knew that Doctor Michaels was the busiest man in the colonies these days, and today would be his busiest yet. There would need to be more help, to get through this. Mentally Mitch made a list of all the personnel he knew who had medical training. It wasn't a long list. Some of the White Collars would, of course, and there seemed to be an endless array of doctors among the First Colony person-alities.

Reilly, he suddenly thought, a flood of worry for her suddenly filling him to the point where he could think of nothing else. He glanced to where he'd left her, and saw a Blue Collar by her side, making sure she was cared for.

Good, Mitch thought. He was going to have to leave her for a while in order to help others. They needed set up a triage for the injured, organize rescue teams, get things in motion because ... *because* ...

He couldn't think. Normally, in a crisis, he could mentally plan every step. Now, though, worry for Reilly filled his brain, leaving little room for anything else.

As Dr. Michaels and another medic arrived to tend to the Captain, Mitch told Janet to get some people started on building a triage. He would have to leave the details to her. He had someone else to tend to, and she was the most important person in the world right now.

Maybe ever.

PENNY AWOKE to the smell of ozone and barbecue. She nearly vomited, once she realized the cause of the smell. Corey had been lifted into the air, held aloft by some strange power wielded by Edward. The same Edward who had shared space in her head for the past few weeks. Corey, in his struggle to escape, had reached out for a cable, and the whole room had gone up in a burst of light.

The room was a disaster now, filled with smoke and roiling mounds of slag metal and scorched wiring. There were small fires everywhere. She and Taggart had used a large piece of equipment for cover, and that was now a ruin of twisted and blackened metal.

She had some scrapes and bruises, and a couple of small burns, mostly on her arms. She was a bit banged up. The last time she felt like this, she'd taken a pretty nasty tumble after losing her grip on a cliff face on Fellor's Colony. Her safety line had saved her from dying, but had done nothing to protect her from being slammed into the cliff wall, sliding down and hitting every jagged edge until she was jerked to a rib-crushing stop. The bruises had taken months to heal. These were worse.

She wobbled to her feet, leaning against the large piece of equipment for balance. She finally noticed Taggart, coming to with a large piece of metal across his legs. She moved to help him, and when she tried to leverage the metal off he cried out.

"I ... I'm pinned pretty good," he said, gasping.

Penny looked closer, trying to peer under the debris. "Are your legs ok? Can you feel them? Wiggle your toes?"

Taggart winced and grunted. "Yes," he said. "Not the most pleasant thing I've done, however."

Penny couldn't help the small smile that broke on her face, and she glanced to make sure Taggart wasn't looking.

He was. But his look was *strange*. He seemed pleased with her, as if he was glad she got his joke, glad she enjoyed it, glad just to have her here.

This was not the Taggart she knew.

The Taggart she knew only used humor to influence and manipulate people, to create good will when he needed something. People laughed with him because they felt doing otherwise would lead to being crushed by the man. He wasn't one, in her experience, to try to break the tension, to keep things calm, to show some small bit of emotion as a means of connecting with someone. He was more like Corey — willing to use any means necessary to get people to do what he wanted.

Corey, she thought.

She stood, looking around the edge of the machinery,

trying to see the spot where, moments ago Corey had been floating, held aloft by the strange energy emitted by Edward.

"Dead," Taggart said from his place on the floor. "He couldn't have survived. That much energy would have turned him to atoms. The other one ..."

"Edward," Penny said absently.

"Edward," Taggart said, and Penny thought she sensed a softness in his voice. "He must have died as well."

Penny looked at the spot a moment longer, then nodded and turned back to Taggart. "We have to get you out of this," she said.

"You might have to go find help," Taggart suggested. "I think it's going to take more than just the two of us."

That was kind, Penny knew. Before, he would have said "more than *you*." He would have looked at her with disdain, thinking of her as a weak *girl*, not a capable woman. He would not have respected her, would not have considered her useful.

She was just about to speak, to say she would go find help, when there was the sound of a young voice from the other side of the machine.

"I can see it," the voice said.

Penny turned and leaned outward, around the edge of the machine, looking cautiously in case something else was about to go wrong.

She saw Edward, floating above the floor by at least two feet. He was surrounded in a nimbus of crackling energy. He was *bright* — enough so that it hurt to look at him. He had not been there a few seconds ago.

"Edward?" Penny said.

Edward didn't move. Instead he stared upward, toward the scarred and burnt ceiling. He was turning slowly, his head moving in an arch, his hands at his side. He was seeing something, though Penny wasn't sure what it could be.

"I can see it *all*," Edward said.

"What, Edward? What do you see?"

The nimbus of energy faded until Edward was easy to look at. Soon he looked — what exactly? Normal? As normal as it was possible to look when you're a young boy floating above the floor.

He turned to Penny. "The paths are beautiful. There are too many to count."

Penny nodded. She wasn't sure what to make of this, but since Edward suddenly seemed more lucid and rational than he had while hitchhiking in her brain, she took that as a very big positive for once.

"Are you ok?" she asked.

Edward said nothing.

"What happened to Corey?" she asked.

"Cowboy was going to hurt you."

Cowboy. Penny had called Corey that as a parting shot before boarding a shuttle to the colony vessel. That seemed so long ago. Years, instead of weeks. She had thought she was being clever, but now she saw she was lighting a fuse. Corey had done the unthinkable, following her here. He planned to hurt her, for certain. He planned to *destroy* her.

Edward knew all of this, of course, being part of her mind after Alan had ...

What? What had Alan done? Where *was* he? Was he ok? Penny couldn't remember anything clearly. She had a vague memory of him falling, maybe from a building or from a shuttle, and she had grabbed him. Her instincts had kicked in, from hundreds of hours of climbing rock faces, and made her act. She had grabbed him and held on until he could climb back to safety.

She could remember all of this a little like remembering a dream. The details were lost, and everything after that was dark and hazy.

"The man is trapped," Edward said, and suddenly he was gone. "I can help him," she heard him say, and she spun around to find him behind her.

Penny gasped. How had he done *that*? How was he doing *any* of it? He'd gone from being a voice in her head to being a ... what? *A real boy*, she thought, but also something more. What was he?

Edward raised his hands slowly, and Taggart gave out a cry of pain. There was the sound of wrenching metal, and Penny watched as the debris slowly rose into the air, freeing Taggart's legs

Penny wasted no time, and rushed to Taggart's side to help him roll away and scoot to safety. The pile of metal then slowly lowered back in place.

"What the hell just happened?" Taggart breathed. He was gripping one of his shins, wincing from pain.

Penny shook her head, wide-eyed. "I have no idea," she said. Edward was something more than she'd expected. She still somehow *felt* him, like a light vibration in the back of her mind. Or maybe that was more like a phantom limb — a tingling sense of where he *used* to be.

She wasn't sure about that, or about anything, except that Edward was more than human. And she couldn't decided if it made her feel afraid or, somehow, proud.

CHAPTER 2

THERE WAS A LOT OF NOISE, AND IT WAS WAKING THOMAS UP — *a big no-no for a Sunday.*

Sundays were his days to sleep in, to take his time getting to the day, to eventually, gradually roll out of bed and check his phone for the latest news, the newest status updates, the top-rated videos. But only when he was ready. Noise was not permitted. He'd have to ...

He'd have to ...

"He's in critical condition, but we just have nowhere to move him. A separate tent is the best we can do, for now. Get those new patients straightened out. Tend the light wounds first. Don't look at me like that, I know protocol. But we have precious few resources here. Stabilize anyone in critical condition, then focus on dressing small wounds and getting those people up off of their butts and in line to help!"

That was weird. That voice was familiar. It was someone Thomas knew, but couldn't quite piece together *how* he knew. *Doctor ... Michaels?* That was it. Kind of a salty old guy. He had one arm in a sling. He was ...

Thomas groaned, and finally opened his eyes. He was in

a tent, which fluttered above him in a breeze. The sounds that had awoken him closed in now, as if the tent were collapsing around him. He saw that he was surrounded by makeshift beds and operating tables, and each was filled with wounded colonists.

He tried to sit up, but someone put a hand on his shoulder to settle him back.

"Take it easy," Doctor Michaels said. "You've been unconscious for the past hour or so. Bad bump to the head. Ease back into it. But don't take too long, we need all hands."

Thomas was obliged to obey. He had a splitting headache, and his neck felt a little wrenched. He was having trouble remembering what happened just before he blacked out.

The wedding.

He tried to sit up again, and managed to get to his elbows. "What happened?" he asked, panicked.

"Explosion," Doctor Michaels said as he finished bandaging a Blue Collar's arm. Once finished, the Blue Collar raced away, presumably to help, and Doctor Michaels busied himself with another patient.

Thomas squeezed the bridge of his nose with his thumb and forefinger. He rubbed his eyes, and tried to relax and let the headache fade and his sore neck muscles unclench, trying to will the headache and pain to subside. It wasn't working.

"What about the others?" he finally asked.

"Some were killed. Some are critically injured. Your friends, Mitch and Reilly, they're ok. Reilly is still unconscious, or was when I last saw her. Mitch Garrison is refusing to leave her side. Which is a shame."

"Why a shame?"

Doctor Michaels looked up, as if he were surprised that

Thomas hadn't figured it out by now. "I need him. The whole damn colony does."

Thomas understood. "Somar ... is he ...?"

Michaels shook his head. "No, not dead. But bad."

So Mitch was the ranking officer, and the colony needed him to take charge. Someone had to step in, give orders, keep the rescue effort going.

One more rescue effort, Thomas thought. *One more explosion. More injured. More dead. How much more of this can we take? How much more can we survive?*

Thomas stood, shrugging off Doctor Michaels and then looking around the room. "Where is Mitch?" Thomas asked.

The Doctor pointed with his good hand before turning back to finish his work.

MITCH WATCHED **Reilly's chest rise and fall**. He couldn't look away. It was as if he were keeping her breathing by his own sheer will, and if he let his focus shift she'd be gone. He wasn't going to move from that spot until she was awake and responsive.

The were in the triage tent, surrounded by dozens of wounded, with more stumbling in all the time. Some were assisted. Most had pulled themselves free. Mitch knew that there were others, trapped and struggling. He knew he should go. He knew that he should get things organized. But instead he sat. He watched Reilly breathe.

"Mitch."

Mitch turned to see Thomas. He stood, staring at Reilly for a moment, then back at Mitch.

"She's hurt," Mitch said, keeping his voice calm.

"Yeah," Thomas said.

Mitch looked back to Reilly, but his mind was now on something else. He knew why Thomas was here. He knew what that look was for. He knew he was needed.

"*You* should do it," Mitch said.

From behind him, he heard Thomas inhale deeply. A sigh, maybe. "I can't, Mitch. You know that. I'm an outsider here. No rank. Some of them might take orders from me, and maybe that would help. But it's not like I'm part of the ECF or anything. I'm not even part of the government here.

"You, though ... you're the ranking officer. The people dealing with this, they're *your* people. Everyone who can be effective at helping the hurt and getting things set back to rights, they're *all* your people. They'll listen to you, without hesitation, and jump when you tell them they have to. Even if they listen to me, I'm just a White Collar to them. They'll waste time. People will die when they could have been saved."

Mitch laughed, bitter. "That's already happened."

"Don't let it *keep* happening."

Mitch nodded. He knew Thomas was right, of course. Knew it, like he knew his own name, like he knew the engines of a shuttle, like he knew the inside of a stasis pod. Still ...

Reilly moved. Mitch suddenly sat up in his chair, and Thomas stepped in beside him. Reilly stirred on the table and finally, slowly, opened her eyes. Mitch felt like he might sob.

"Mitch," she said, her voice small and scuffed sounding.

Mitch laughed, but felt warmth and wet in his eyes. Thomas also laughed, and put a hand on Mitch's shoulder.

They explained the mess, the explosion and the aftermath. Mitch waited for Thomas to say something, to hint that it was time to leave, time to go *lead*. But to his credit, he said nothing.

It was Reilly who spoke.

"You need to go," she said.

Mitch, caught off guard, shook his head. "No ... no I need to be *here*."

"Come on," Reilly said. "Since when? I married the guy who would be out there right now, making sure everyone was taken care of. You need to *go*."

Mitch was confused, then a little angry. He started to open his mouth, probably just to stick his foot in, he knew. But he caught himself. What was *really* holding him back? Reilly was right. Thomas was right. The Blue Collars were the best qualified to help in this situation, but they needed someone out there coordinating their efforts, making tough calls, giving orders and direction. Right now, everyone was doing the best they could, but they weren't working as a team. Not yet. Mitch knew exactly what they needed. He knew what *he* needed.

He needed to go.

He turned to Thomas, but was holding Reilly's hand. "I'm going," he said.

Thomas nodded. Reilly squeezed his hand, when he looked she was smiling. "That's my guy," she said, and then drifted back to sleep.

Mitch would have moved a mountain after that, if she just hinted she wanted him to.

Which was good. Because as he stood, as Thomas promised he would keep an eye on her, moving a mountain — one made of smoldering and twisted metal — was exactly what Mitch was preparing to do.

ALAN WAS DOING HIS BEST, **but there were trust issues.** In an emergency, it seemed, a lot of things could be forgiven and forgotten. But not completely, and not all at once.

The guards were still with him, still watching him, but had apparently decided he was *needed* out here. It may have had something to do with Somar being in critical condition, and everyone else being more or less out of commission.

Alan helped with some of the rescue effort before realizing there had to be a better and safer way. They were man-handling chunks of debris out of the way, pulling people free as gingerly and safely as they could. But the work was going too slow. The volume of debris, the weight of it and its instability, were forcing them to move at a pace that might cost lives.

Alan knew that he wasn't much use as muscle. They needed every bicep they could get, of course, but short of just throwing himself into the physical effort there had to be a way he could help in a more effective manner. He was thinking about this, and about the hazards of the work in which they were engaged, when a thought suddenly occurred to him.

"I think we can use one of the repulsors," Alan said out of the blue.

The others working with him were primarily Blue Collar mechanics and service techs. They were used to heavy lifting, but were also used to having tools to help. Alan started talking, as he kept up the work, about making a quick modification to a shuttle's atmospheric stabilizer, one of the repulsor engines, and using it more or less like a crane to lift debris gently out of the way. "We would be able to lift greater weight with that," he said. "We could clear this stuff faster, get to more people sooner."

The team generally liked the idea. "But we can't stop,"

one of the Blue Collars said sternly. "We don't have time for this, Alan."

Alan nodded. "We should keep working. But if I could take a couple of people, just to help gather materials, we could grab one of the spare stabilizers brought back from the platform. I believe I could modify it in about half an hour. It might save us days of removing debris — days in which some of these people may die."

There was chatter. As expected, some of them objected to letting him make the call. Others were worried about the prospect of letting him have access to technology, after what he'd done. Still others argued that since the explosion, Alan had worked tirelessly to help in the rescue effort.

In the end, reluctant but short on options, they decided to give him a shot. The guards went with him, and helped him gather tools and parts. Soon, within fifteen minutes, Alan had a makeshift workbench set up and was cobbling together what he hoped would be a "repulsor crane."

A short time later he had something he felt would work. He and the guards quickly placed it in front of a large chunk of debris, already cleared from the wreckage. Alan aimed, made some adjustments, and then triggered the repulsor with a swipe on his handheld.

The debris suddenly flew upward, air whistling around it as it launched into the sky.

Alan and the guards stood, jaws open, as it disappeared into the clouds.

"I really hope that doesn't come back down on us," one of the guards said.

Alan quickly tapped commands into the handheld and brought up data from the remaining Citadel sensors. For extra measure he added in sensor data from the grounded shuttles all around them. "It's ok," Alan said, sighing in relief and allowing himself to smile a little. "It's in geosync."

"It's in *orbit*?" one of the guards said.

The other guard huffed a laugh. Alan, shaking his head, said, "I made a small error. I can fix that. But this is good. It works. Sort of. Let's get going. We've wasted enough time on testing."

The guards nodded, then helped Alan carry the repulsor and some other equipment back to where the rescue team was still manhandling debris.

Alan was nervous as he set up, but after a moment the calm came back. He was feeling what he always felt when building something, when he was programming or finding and fixing bugs. It was a sort of serenity, a sort of *zen*. Everything that had happened recently just fell away — all the betrayals, all the chaos, all the deaths and injuries. Alan saw only the task at hand. In moments, he had the crane ready.

"You're sure we're not about to fling someone into space?" one of the guards said.

Others looked shocked and concerned, and in answer Alan simply aimed the device and turned it on.

The large, impossibly heavy chunk of metal that had been a barrier for the past few hours suddenly rose into the air, as if floating on a gentle air current. It hovered at about six feet, and Alan tapped a few instructions into the control system. The debris shuddered in mid air, then glided to a spot several feet away, clear of the area.

There was a quick cheer before rescue team rushed in and started tossing smaller bits of wreckage aside, crying out as they found injured in the rubble. Before long there was a carry line, moving the wounded out and to safety.

Alan breathed easier, collapsing a little and leaning on the repulsor's housing. He had been afraid, if he was being honest. Not that his plan wouldn't work, or that his machine would fail. He had instead been afraid that his effort would cost precious time, that people would die. He was afraid that he would cause more harm than good, as he had for so long now.

He was afraid that he really *was* the villain. It was a relief, then, to discover that he might not be after all.

THOMAS MADE sure Reilly was comfortable and recovering before leaving her side. It was the least he could do for Mitch, and for her. He owed them quite a lot, he knew. But there was someone else he needed to see now.

Doctor Michaels accompanied him into the separate tent where Somar was resting.

"I have him on life support, though I can't tell how effective it is. His physiology isn't that different from ours, in general terms at least. I can keep his heart going. I just can't tell if he's got a shot at recovery."

"What about ..." Thomas hesitated. He wasn't sure how much Doctor Michaels knew about Somar's "abilities." The Captain had entrusted that secret to Thomas in a blood bond. But now, as Thomas stared at his friend, laced with tubes and wires, attached to machines doing their best to keep him alive, he wasn't sure if such a secret had any place here.

"Doctor, how much *do* you know about Esool physiology?"

Michaels shrugged. "As much as any Earth Fleet doctor, really. I know their genome is plant based. And I know they have a metabolism that makes ours look like a slug racing a shuttle."

Again Thomas hesitated, and then said, "But what about healing?"

Doctor Michaels looked at him sidelong. "You know, then."

Thomas nodded. "Somar shared it with me on our fist day here. He healed my hands."

"I wondered about that. I think I knew that, actually."

"So you know that he can heal others? And heal himself?"

"It's come up, but I was placed under oath, told never to reveal that knowledge or face perjury charges, maybe even a court marshal, though I'm not technically in the military. I guess none of that matters now, though. And you obviously know all about it."

"I wouldn't say *all* about it. But I'm not sure what good it does us. Somar told me that his people could heal someone who was severely injured, but takes a consolidated effort — several Esool, all sharing their blood. One Esool wouldn't be able to heal someone with this level of injury. I was hoping you might know a way to boost the effect."

Doctor Michaels shook his head. "No, I have no idea how to do that. I'm aware of how they heal in groups, but I don't know how to amplify the effect of the blood. It's a holy grail in the medical community right now. At least, it is to those of us who know about it. But it would take a tremendous amount of blood to ..."

Michaels stopped in his tracks, causing Thomas to look closer. "What is it?"

"I can't believe I didn't think of this before. But, dammit, there are some complications. Of course there are."

"Complications? What's happening? What did you remember?"

Instead of answering, Doctor Michaels gestured for

Thomas to follow, and the two of them left the tent and made their way across the compound. The rescue effort was still in full effect, but the frenetic activity was starting to slow. Thomas had heard rumors, that Alan had stepped up with some kind of invention, and it was making all the difference. *Good*, Thomas thought. It might not be enough, especially for those who suffered great losses here, but it was a start.

Michaels led him into the small building that was known as the "hospital" for the colony. It would be filled to capacity right now, Thomas knew. But one small room was all but empty. At its center was one stasis pod, with another was resting against a far wall among a collection of medical equipment.

Thomas peered through the transparent window of the first pod and saw Captain Alonzo inside, his face scarred and burned, but otherwise serene and at peace. Thomas shuddered involuntarily.

"He's in very bad shape," Michaels said.

"Will he survive?" Thomas asked.

The doctor checked the pod's readout, tapping the display a few times to bring up biometric data. He somewhat subconsciously shook his head, though Thomas didn't believe he was saying "no." It felt more like "unlikely."

"He's in critical condition, of course. If he weren't in stasis, he'd be dead already. As it is, treating him is next to impossible. Bringing him out of stasis long enough to administer aid will likely kill him. But Somar had a plan."

Thomas looked at him with surprise. "Something to do with his blood?"

"He was stockpiling it," Michaels said, then led Thomas to the second stasis pod.

Thomas peered inside, but couldn't quite make anything

out. There was no one in there, but he could see hundreds of small metal cylinders.

"Blood," Michaels said. "For some time now Somar has had as much of it drawn as he could. He would then bathe and feed, and whatever else he does to replenish his blood supply. He spent a lot of time at the river, where that idiot Jack died."

Thomas had heard about the mutiny, and knew that Somar had more or less revealed his abilities to everyone, there by the river. Though it was certain that most were aware that Somar could heal himself, they likely would not assume he could heal others. That was good, because if word got out that Somar's blood could heal humans the alien Captain would likely be torn to shreds, in the name of treating the wounded among the colonists. And there were always wounded.

"So he was stockpiling blood to heal Alonzo. Would that work?"

"It might," Michaels shrugged. "But Somar planned to draw much more than what we have. Alonzo's living on borrowed time, and his check is due. He won't survive coming out of stasis, not without a miracle. Somar was trying to grow a miracle."

Thomas nodded. He was starting to understand what Michaels was doing. In effect, he was asking Thomas to give an order. "You want me to choose between Alonzo and Somar."

"More than that," Michaels said. "That stockpile of blood could heal some of the humans here as well. I don't know how far it could stretch, but it could be useful. The question is, do we kill the goose to get to the golden eggs?"

Thomas blinked. "I hadn't thought of it like that. It's kind of ... it feels *wrong*, somehow. Do we save Somar, just to make him a ... what — a medicine factory?"

Michaels shrugged. "Ethics. But this goes beyond anything I've ever had to deal with in the course of my career. I can't answer it, I can only point it out. Somar would have to decide. But he's incapacitated. Someone is going to have to make the decision for him. And that someone will have to be you."

Thomas was surprised. "Why me?"

"Somar informed me weeks ago that as far as 'next of kin,' you're the closest he has."

After thinking about that, Thomas felt a little light-headed. *Blood brothers*, he thought. After healing his injuries, Somar had told Thomas that they now shared a bond of blood. That made Thomas family, in a sense. He had the right to make the call.

"You need to make your decision pretty quick," Michaels said. "Time isn't on our side."

Thomas nodded. He felt numb. But he knew, deep down, what the answer would be. It couldn't be anything else, he realized. He had to make the choice that Somar himself would make, if he were here. He had to make a choice that would save the most people. And that choice meant at least one man would die.

"Do it," Thomas said. "Use the blood, and heal Somar. We need him."

Michaels nodded, though he seemed grim.

As the two of them left the room, Thomas glanced back at Alonzo's pod.

It looks like a casket, Thomas thought. *Or maybe I just made it one.*

CHAPTER 3

IT WAS WEIRD SEEING EDWARD LEVITATE THINGS OUT OF THE way. Though if Penny were being honest with herself, it was weird seeing Edward at all. The boy who had been a hitch-hiker in her brain was now some kind of ... what exactly? A superhero, like from the vids?

He could hover above the floor, he could wield some weird energy, he could move things without touching them — that sure fit the part.

He was also somehow more coherent than he had been before. Penny knew, from their shared memories and from various bits of overheard conversation she could remember —Edward was autistic. She didn't know much about the condition, but did know that it usually meant someone was mentally disabled. Or was that the right word? She wasn't sure Edward could ever have been called *disabled*. If anything, his mind was *more enabled*. He was obsessed with details that most "normal" people could ignore. His only shortcoming, basically, was that he had trouble interacting with people.

But the boy hovering before her and Taggart seemed

anything *but* autistic. He seemed incredibly alert, if a bit quiet. He was *contemplative* ... that was the word. He was capable. He was a little frightening.

He cleared a path for them as they went, opening pathways through the wreckage of the tower, letting them cut in more or less a straight line to the outside.

Penny felt a sense of dread about the state of the tower. Citadel was sort of their lifeline, here in the colony. It had been a kind of comfort to see, as she roamed around in a haze. She could remember it, even though most of her memories were a bit foggy. It had gleamed, she knew. It had patterns of bolts and wires and conduits. More importantly, it *stood* for something — it had meaning among the colonists, especially after Somar had made a speech about them all being a family.

That speech had made its way to everyone in the colony, to the point where even those who hadn't been there remembered it as if they were. A central image of that speech had been Citadel, standing tall and gleaming in the sunlight of this strange world where none of them belonged. And now the tower was wreckage. What would that mean to the colony?

They broke through, finally, to the outside. Taggart was hobbling along, leaning on Penny for support, with his arm around her shoulder. Penny was mostly ok, though she had some burns and bruises. Edward, on the other hand, was ...

Perfect, Penny thought.

He glowed with energy, even though he'd suppressed the most outward sign of it. It was gentle, a sort of Gaussian blur to his skin. It made him look flawless and perfect. Penny had never seen his face before today, but remembered it in scattered swatches of memory, glances in mirrors from when he was a child on earth. She remembered that well enough that she could tell he was a more refined version of himself. This body he wore wasn't real.

When they were outside, in the sunlight and the cooling afternoon air, Penny gasped at what she saw.

"My God," Taggart whispered beside her.

The scene before them looked like a war zone. Chunks of ragged and torn metal were strewn all over, and people were busily moving bits of it, helping others to stand or carrying them out of the wreckage to medical care.

The scene was chaotic, and felt completely unorganized.

She was about to ask Taggart what he thought they should do, when suddenly she saw a face she recognized.

Alan, surrounded by a handful of others, was setting up a machine. Penny watched as Alan activated it, and a large section of the Citadel tower rose several feet into the air before gently floating aside.

Penny had watched Edward perform this same trick numerous times now, but it was somehow more impressive to see it done by Alan's machine. What Edward did through some weird superpower, Alan did with tools he designed and built, using nothing but what he had at hand. And that, for some reason, made it more impressive.

She felt a mixture of emotions. She was aware, some-how, that Alan was responsible for everything that had happened to them — to *her* — over the past few weeks. She could remember snatches of conversation about him, about his *betrayal*.

But she also remembered his kindness and attentive-ness. He was quiet, and so very, very smart. He was kind of a geek, really, and Penny usually wouldn't have time for a guy like him. But something about him had gotten to her. She remembered his eyes, his voice, the feel of his hand in hers, helping her stand when they were done resting out in the wilds. She remembered him falling from a shuttle, and her grabbing *his* hand, to save him.

She was thinking about what to do next, about the best way to approach him, when Taggart said, "What's he doing?"

She noticed, then, that Edward was gently gliding away from them, toward Alan and his machine.

Enough, she said, shaking her head to clear it of all the confusion, all the questions she had. Plenty of time for questions. For now, it was time to help.

MITCH KNEW **he had to get his head straight.**

Reilly is ok. Reilly is ok.

It became his mantra as he walked, and it punctuated the silence between commands as he organized Blue Collars and White Collars into teams.

Rescue was well under way. Doctor Michaels had the triage under control, moving less critical patients out of the way, sometimes flat-out enlisting them to help with critical care. Casualties were higher than Mitch would have liked, but that was a given. Now, right now, was about minimizing any further casualties, and giving everyone some direction and hope.

The problem was all the damned metal.

Mitch did a quick visual assessment of the Citadel tower. The explosion had to have happened in Citadel's main engine room. It was the only part of the tower that had enough stored energy to cause this much damage. The structural framework of the tower was more or less intact — it still rose into the sky, though a large portion at its base bulged outward in knots of twisted and melted metal.

The debris that had fallen on top of them largely consisted of the modular components, meant for cannibalization and conversion into housing and other resources.

It would mean a hit to their building progress, as materials would now be even more scarce or would require more tooling and repair. But with so many critically injured or dead, building materials were the least of their worries at the moment.

It was amazing that any of Citadel still stood, but there it was, winding up into the sky, metal blackened by fire, parts molten and twisted, but still standing. It hurt his heart to see it in that condition. Over the past few weeks he had come to see it as so man others had — a symbol of hope, and of the strength of the colony. The damage, severe as it was, seemed to hint at weakness and corruption within them all. It told a story that was less about hope and more about tragedy.

But it could be fixed. Just about *anything* could be fixed, with enough materials, enough talent, enough pure human brilliance. They had those things in spades. The people of this colony had pulled together more than once. They were getting good at it. Given time, they would rebuild, both this tower and the hope it stood for.

Time was the part that worried Mitch. It seemed to be running short for all of them.

Which was why Mitch had to force himself to focus on the immediate challenges and let things play out however they would play out. And at the moment, all this metal was a problem that Mitch had to figure a way to solve.

Moving all of this by hand was too slow, and in some cases impossible. There were chunks of heavy metal that were large enough to make them impossible to move with manpower alone.

Maybe they could use the shuttles — air lift some of the

debris away. The danger there was that it lacked precision. They could do more harm than good, if they weren't careful. More people could die.

Still, there had to be a ... way ... "What the *hell*?"

Mitch had just given orders for two of his engineers to clear a more direct path to the hospital when he saw a large chunk of debris suddenly float upward, then glide gently to the side. From his vantage point, he watched as the metal rose out of the way, revealing a group of people on the other side, apparently using a modified shuttle repulsor engine to clear the debris. Mitch was impressed by the ingenuity. This was exactly the kind of brilliance he'd come to expect! It was a sign of hope that someone had not only had the presence of mind to think through the problem, they had the brains to create a real solution. He was already going over to find out who it was, to praise and congratulate them, when he stopped short.

There, at the controls, was Alan Angelou.

Mitch felt his face go hot and a rush of pressure in his temples and behind his eyes. Before he had fully processed everything he was seeing, he already had a wrench in his hand and was striding toward Alan and the others. He wasn't sure what he was about to do, but he knew exactly why he was *angry*.

Alan was the cause of all of this.

The ship crashing, people dying, *Reilly hurt*. All of the suffering of the past few weeks could be traced directly back to Alan.

Mitch was closing in, wrench in hand, when he caught movement off to the right. He glanced that way as he moved, and then came to a sudden halt.

At first he thought that maybe Alan's modification to the

repulsor was still operating — but the object floating above the ground wasn't a piece of debris.

It was a *child*.

A boy, around 13 years old by the look of him, was gliding over the ground toward Alan and the others. Following close behind him was another strange sight — Penny, now apparently back to normal, was helping Taggart to cross the gap between Citadel and Alan's group.

Perhaps it was the succession of double takes, but Mitch suddenly realized that, seconds earlier, he'd been on his way to do some serious damage to Alan's skull. He still felt a bit angry, if he was honest. He wanted to hold someone accountable for all of this, wanted to *punish* someone for hurting Reilly. But that couldn't be Alan, he realized. Not this way, at any rate. If he was punished, it would be under the rule of law. Doing things outside of the rules was Alan's way, not Mitch's.

He let the wrench drop, heard it clang to the ground, and accepted that as the sound of his own anger falling away. Alan should see justice, but that wasn't Mitch's call. For now, there was something strange happening, and Mitch found that he was more curious about this floating boy than he was angry about Alan's part in all of this.

He resumed walking toward them all.

ALAN WASN'T sure what he was seeing, at first.

There was a boy, floating above the ground. Seconds ago he had used the "repulsor crane" to levitate a large chunk of metal out of the way. Were the two connected? He checked the controls on the repulsor — it was powered down.

The boy was intriguing enough to get Alan's attention,

but then he saw something that drove all other thoughts and curiosities away.

Penny Daunder was walking toward him, and with her was Alan's father.

Or rather, it was the man who had been the *host* of Alan's father, before the Current apparently removed the wave-form. Alan had realized it just before the explosion, but had not had much time to think about it since.

Somehow, these three strange things together — the boy, Penny, Taggart — made a kind of sense to Alan, though he could never explain why.

He felt a slight buzz and tingling on the skin of his fore-arms as the boy came closer. He recognized it as ambient energy, similar to what you would feel when standing close to a live transformer. He'd felt it before, he realized, though not quite as intensely. Earlier, when the Current had used one of the colonists as a host, there had been a consistent, low-grade tingle of electricity in the air.

The instruments were able to detect it, so Alan knew it was more than imagination. The Current, whatever else it might be, was an energy-based life form. It had the ability to see and interact with other energy fields, including the energy comprising human thoughts. It had, somehow, removed the suppression waveform that allowed Alan's father to live again, using Taggart's body.

Alan felt a pang of sadness over that. He missed his father terribly, and the past few weeks were the closest he'd come to seeing him again. He'd *communicated* with him, through Taggart, and had the chance to know him again after so many years. And now his father was gone again. Maybe forever.

No time for that now, Alan thought. There were plenty of mysteries to solve, right here in this small cluster of humans, amid the debris of the Citadel tower. There were mysteries within mysteries.

"Alan," Penny said quietly. She was supporting Taggart, who was limping and having trouble standing.

Alan felt his stomach clench. Penny's tone wasn't icy, but it was cautious, guarded. She'd lost trust in him, he could tell. She was wary. And she was right.

Again Alan felt the weight of everything he'd done. This ... *all* of this ... was ultimately his fault. He'd been obsessed with fixing everything, after *First Colony*. He'd been obsessed with redeeming Uncle John. But mostly he'd been obsessed with cheating death, with bringing his parents back to life.

And, in a way, he had succeeded — the personalities of those original colonists now lived again, in the minds of the people from this colony. They walked and thought and talked again, a century after the terrorist act that had killed them all. It had been a miracle, and Alan had done it against all odds.

But the cost was too high. In trying to right a great wrong, he'd brought more harm and hurt to thousands of innocents. In all of his plans and calculations and strategies, in his obsession to restore the lives of the lost, he had forgotten about the lives he'd affect in trade. Lives like hers.

"Penny," he said, also quiet and cautious, silently asking for ... what, exactly? Forgiveness? Hope? Too much by far. More than he deserved.

He turned to Taggart. "Are you ok, Mr. Taggart? Do you need to see a doctor?"

Taggart winced but straightened himself a bit. "I'll be fine. There are people in greater need." Alan thought this was the sort of thing Taggart would have said, weeks ago, as a show for caring about others. Now, however, it sounded more like his father. It sounded *genuine*. Taggart was looking closely at him, "How did you know it was me and not your father?"

Alan took a deep breath before speaking, letting it calm him. "I realized it after you left the lab. Our scans of the host indicated that things had changed and the Current wasn't in control of him anymore. That and the fact that you were a little disoriented when you left made me suspicious, but I knew for sure when I saw you. Small things are different. Mannerisms. Something in your eyes." Alan shrugged at this point, unsure what else he should say.

Taggart nodded, and said nothing, which, again, was oddly reminiscent of Alan's father.

Alan turned now to the boy, who was indeed levitating above the ground. Alan suspected he wasn't actually a boy at all, but maybe some sort of hologram. "You're the Current," he said.

"I am Edward," the boy said, but after a pause added "*and* the Current."

Alan considered this and was about to respond when a voice came from behind him. "Did you cause this explosion?"

Alan and the others turned to see Mitch Garrison, standing with his hands firmly at his side, as if he had to force them to stay there. Alan felt a deep sting when he saw his friend ... his *former* friend ... obviously angry and fighting to restrain himself.

Alan wished he wouldn't. He suddenly wanted very much for Mitch to strike out, to punch him, to beat him until he was bleeding and unconscious on the ground.

Of all of his betrayals, the two biggest were Penny and Mitch. Alan had never cared much about how people felt about him, had never felt particularly close to anyone before, but these two ...

Edward didn't turn his head so much as rotate in mid air to face Mitch. "Yes," he answered, accepting responsibility for the explosion that had torn through the colony, had injured most and killed many, and had abruptly ended the most joyful day of Mitch's life.

Alan felt a sudden dread, and in a flash wondered about Reilly. Was she alive? Was she injured? Before he could ask he saw Mitch tense and take a small, involuntary step toward Edward.

"No!" Penny said, stepping between Mitch and the boy. "No, he did *not* cause it. Not directly. It was Corey!"

"Who is Corey?" Mitch asked, halting but never taking his eyes off of Edward.

"Corey?" said Wilson, one of the Blue Collars who had been working with Alan to clear debris. "*The* Corey? The vid star?"

This seemed to shake Mitch loose a bit. "Vid star? What?"

"I saw him around the colony," Wilson said. "He's been here for a couple of weeks now, I think."

"He was trying to ... hurt me," Penny said, glancing quickly at Taggart who nodded, confirming. "Edward stopped him. He lifted him into the air," she waved at Edward's feet, levitating several inches above the ground. "Corey started flailing and grabbed some kind of cable."

"He was highly charged," Taggart said to Mitch. "Edward apparently controls some sort of electrical energy. When Corey touched one of the primary conduits the whole engine went up. We barely survived."

Mitch took this in, glancing occasionally at Edward but

primarily looking from Penny to Taggart as they spoke, his expression unreadable.

Then, as if the whole matter were settled, he said, "We still have work to do." He turned and issued orders to the Blue Collars and White Collars, getting them started on using the modified repulsor to lift and remove debris, telling them to take any injured to the triage area.

Orders given, he then turned Alan. "You're going back to your cell."

"Wait, what?" Wilson said. "Mitch, it was Alan who ..."

"Get to work," Mitch told Wilson before turning and walking away.

The two guards somewhat reluctantly took Alan by the arms and guided him toward the lab where he'd spent the past few days. Alan made no attempt to resist. If his modifications to the repulsor were working, then he'd done all he could do for the colony here. Now it was time to get back to his real work — figuring out a way to undo all of the damage he'd caused here.

Suddenly he had an idea. He turned his head slightly, "Penny! Bring the Current to my lab!"

Penny looked from Alan to Taggart and back again. "Who? Where?"

"Edward! Bring Edward."

"I know where," Taggart said.

And then Alan was out of earshot.

THINGS WERE GOING VERY WELL for the Chairman, as things generally did. This time, however, he was particularly pleased with his success.

Rudford had delivered a very promising lead —

someone in a crucial role in Taggart's network. Someone over whom Taggart had leverage, and therefore the Chairman would have leverage.

The Chairman sat at his large desk, sucking on a butterscotch candy as a man named O'Neill quietly fidgeted and sweat in the chair opposite.

"O'Neill," the Chairman said. "Your family founded Imminent Technologies."

O'Neill started to speak but apparently his throat was dry. He gave a rough and pitched false start, cleared his throat with a cough, and started again. "Yes. I inherited the company when my father died four years ago."

"As well as your family's wealth, it would seem."

"Yes," O'Neill said. The Chairman noted a slight flush to the man's skin, a quick glance to the side. *Shame*. The Chairman knew why O'Neill would be ashamed — knew *all* the reasons. Only some of which had to do with losing his family's wealth in bad investments. The "investments" themselves would be the biggest source of shame.

"Things are not going so well, are they, Mr. O'Neill?"

There was a subconscious and subtle shaking of the head before O'Neill responded in an amiable tone. "We had a rough patch, but we're recovering well, thanks to a few well-timed investments and some new holdings."

Well-timed investments. New holdings. The only investment was Taggart's interest, and the new holding was Taggart's grip on the man and his wealth.

The Chairman waited and watched as the man assumed his deception was taken at face value. In the uncomfortable silence, O'Neill spoke again. "We're actually making great strides in advancing lightrail technology. Our engineering teams are innovating into new ..."

"O'Neill, please do not waste my time. I find it displeasing."

O'Neill stuttered a bit, but recovered. The Chairman saw a small fire rise in the man. He was not accustomed to being interrupted or commanded, especially by someone he'd only just met. In his small world, O'Neill was in charge. He called the shots. *He* did the interrupting.

But not here. Not now. Not ever again.

"I have paid a great sum of money to find you, O'Neill. Do you know why?"

O'Neill blinked, and opened his mouth to say something, but apparently thought better of it and simply shook his head.

"You have ties to this organization, do you not?"

"Earth First? I ... yes, I do. I was ... recruited."

"By Taggart?"

"By one of his *representatives*," O'Neill said, and the Chairman picked up on a minute shudder and the slight note of fear and revulsion in the man's voice. The Chairman assumed that Taggart must have an associate who functioned in similar capacity as Rudford. Unfortunate for O'Neill. Unfortunate for the associate, as well. He would need to be found an eliminated. The Chairman noted this with a few taps, knowing that Rudford would have this associate's name and location by the end of the hour, and that the problem would find itself resolved in a day or so.

"But you have since met with Taggart."

O'Neill nodded.

The Chairman leaned back, his chair creaking under his weight. His massive hands were still resting on the desk, as if he might pick it up and hurl it at O'Neill at any moment. In fact, the Chairman could do just that. He prided himself on his great strength, though he rarely displayed it. There was little need.

He knew the effect he had on people. He was a large man, always had been. When leaning forward he could seem menacing, but still human, still vulnerable. When he sat up —rising to his fill height, shoulders broadening, chest expanding — his vulnerability was replaced with intimidating girth and mass. The full width of his thick shoulders became visible, his chest expanded to the point that the buttons threatened to pop and fly from his shirt like projectiles. He was a powerful beast rising to its full height, towering over anyone before him, even as he merely sat behind his desk. It never failed to intimidate.

It helped that he'd had the office specially designed to accentuate his size. His desk and chair were slightly smaller than they appeared to be, and the guest's chair slightly larger. A small, cleverly hidden platform lifted his chair by nearly half an inch just as he took his seat, rising slowly enough that it went unnoticed, and instead gave the impression that he was somehow growing *larger* before the eyes of anyone seated before him.

The windows behind him — actually vid screens that could change configuration and scenery on his command — curved in slightly from the top. At the moment they were set to resemble five tall and narrow windows, like a stubbed hand made of bright light in an otherwise darkened wall. It gave the impression that the room was grasping, reaching toward the observer, closing in on whomever happened to be sitting and facing that direction. The proportions of the room, in general, were off by such a slight degree that it created an instinctive sense of uneasiness in anyone who entered.

This room was built for intimidation.

"When Taggart's people first approached you, it was because your company was failing. I have that information from my man Rudford. I also have some very interesting data about *why* it was failing. Would you care to hear it?"

O'Neill swallowed. "No, that's fine. I'm aware."

"As was Taggart, it seems," the Chairman said, affecting a mock tone of sympathy. "He had you fairly well entangled, with threats to you and even your family. I am aware of how ... *aggressive* ... Taggart can be."

O'Neill was nodding, perhaps subconsciously.

The Chairman knew exactly what sort of methods and pressures Taggart was capable of deploying. In many ways they were very much alike. The Chairman even admired Taggart, in small measure. He was capable, ruthless, driven ... all traits that the Chairman valued and shared. But this insistence on running his own agenda, outside the bounds of the organization — it had finally become too much to tolerate. For his transgressions, Taggart must finally pay a penalty. A rather steep one.

"Mr. O'Neill," the Chairman said, leaning forward once again, becoming human once again. "I would like to help you."

The reaction was immediate, though subtle. O'Neill, only seconds before intimidated to the point of breaking, reminded of the leverage that Taggart had over him and the hopelessness of his situation, suddenly flashed with hope. "Help me? How?"

The Chairman smiled, which he knew did little to soften his features. Rudford — one of the few the Chairman could trust to voice his opinion without fear — had once described him as appearing to be a great beast baring fangs, showing his victims the gateway to their final destination. The

Chairman liked this description so much that he had his teeth modified, ever so slightly, to make them appear sharper and faintly pointed. Again, it was a subtle effect, but potent.

It was not wasted on O'Neill. Instantly, his expression of hope changed to one of dread and fear. The Chairman's message was clear, in one expression. *I want to help you, as long as you are useful to me.*

When the Chairman spoke, however, he was genial, "You have a prominent position in Taggart's network. Your company creates components that are integral to the lightrail hubs. As I understand it, you are fully aware of Taggart's plan to seize control of the lightrail?"

"I ... yes. But I ..."

The Chairman raised one of his massive hands, waving off O'Neill's attempt to explain his link to Taggart's treason. "I do not care about your culpability in the plan, O'Neill. What I care about is your role. You would aid Taggart in seizing control of the lightrail, and you would be rewarded with freedom. I assume he intended to let you take up residence on his moon, or one of the remote colonies, where you would escape the consequences of your crimes. You would live out the rest of your days being served by others, knowing that Taggart's control of the lightrail would prevent anyone from reaching you to mete out any form of punishment."

O'Neill was suddenly very pale. Rudford's intelligence gathering was beyond reproach, as always. The Chairman knew, from O'Neill's reaction, that this was absolutely accurate. It was all the confirmation he needed. "You will continue your operation as Taggart has commanded."

O'Neill blinked, sputtered a bit, and finally managed to respond. "But ... he wants to *shut down* the entire lightrail.

That would essentially give him control of the colonies. Are you saying you want that?"

"The colonies are meaningless to me, O'Neill. As they should be to *any* member of Earth First." He stared hard at the man, marveling at how someone could become even more pale. There must surely be no blood left in him from the neck up.

"I will ensure that your receive your ... *reward*. Frankly, someone with your *appetites* should be as far from this world as you can be." Again O'Neill flinched, as if struck by the Chairman's words. "In return for our honoring of Taggart's deal, you will continue with Taggart's plan, with one exception. From this point forward, you will report directly to Rudford. All information, all communications, all findings. I want to know who else is playing a role in this plan. I want to know the specifics of how Taggart intends to control the network. He is too clever to leave it entirely to you, and therefore he must have other lackeys."

O'Neill's blood rose again, apparently in reaction to being called a "lackey." But he said nothing, which marked him as far wiser than the Chairman had credited him to be.

Instead, he nodded. It was more a weak gesture of submission than one of agreement.

"Very good. Rudford will show you out."

O'Neill's expression changed to fear again, if only for a brief flash, but again he nodded. Rudford entered, having been just outside the door, listening to the conversation. He stood close to O'Neill as the man rose, a bit shakily, and walked out of the Chairman's office.

The Chairman smiled, and consulted the surface of his desk, where a document was displayed. Rudford's research had uncovered a very detailed and convoluted plan. Taggart's network was vast. He had clearly used Earth First as a recruitment tool, caring little for the organization's mission or objectives. He had infiltrated the organization with his own people as a means of keeping his personal network organized. That was his mistake, and it would be his downfall. There was no colony world where he would be safe from Earth First, or from the Chairman.

Clearing the screen, he reached into the small wooden box for another butterscotch. Unwrapping it, he popped it into his mouth and then twisted the yellow plastic wrapper into a slender string. This he held up to catch and reflect the light from the windows behind him. And as it glowed, appearing to hover in space as it was held from the tips of his fingers, he quickly crumpled it into his palm and tossed it aside, letting it fall into the darkness of his office floor, where someone would eventually sweep it away.

THOMAS WAS BANDAGED AND BRUISED. *Again.*

It was becoming a little too common. Over the past few weeks he'd been burned, banged up, cut, scraped, and knocked around more than he could remember. He'd also been miraculously healed at one point, which was a sharp reminder of the task ahead.

He had insisted on being in the room when Dr. Michaels did the procedure. If he was going to sentence one man to death while saving another, he was going to be a part of it from start to finish. No waiting in the halls, no distracting himself until the work was done, no pretending that he was following a moral or ethical imperative. He wasn't at all sure he'd made the right choice.

The colony needed Somar. Despite some lingering racism, many of the humans had come to recognize Somar as a source of leadership and strength. He was, in many ways, a symbol of hope for the colony. Losing him, after every other blow they'd taken, would set them back. It might be the one thing that toppled the whole house of cards.

But losing Captain Alonzo ... wouldn't that be equally as devastating?

Thomas reminded himself, again, that most of these people assumed Alonzo was already dead, lost to them along with everything else on that orbital platform. There would be many who knew he was alive and in stasis, based on rumors if nothing else. But with everything they'd gone through, and with Alonzo's absence in the day-to-day running of things, most people had subconsciously counted him among the lost.

Somar was intent on saving him, Thomas thought.

It was true. Somar had gone to extraordinary lengths in a plan to heal Alonzo, using Somar's own blood. He may have done it out of a sense of decency and empathy, but Thomas didn't think so. Knowing Somar as he did, Thomas was pretty sure the Captain did little that wasn't part of some overall strategy for the good of the colony. If he was trying to save Alonzo, it was likely for more than just the "humanity" of the situation. Somar *knew* something, or had planned something, or maybe just *suspected* something.

Whatever Somar's reasons, Thomas was about to unravel his plans from the inside. Because despite trusting Somar completely, all Thomas had to go by was his own insight, his own knowledge, and his own sense of responsibility. His own gut.

As far as he could determine, the greater need of the colony was the alien Captain, who could inspire even those who hated and feared him. And who, incidentally, had the ability to heal people with his blood. There might come a time when that made the difference in the colony's survival.

Dr. Michaels and an assistant had removed the canisters of blood and emptied them into a large, inflatable vat. Thomas thought it looked somewhat like an inflatable swimming pool that kids would play in, only it was made of a tough, grey material that was incredibly durable as well as being air and water tight. It rose like a volcano, wide at its base and narrowing at the top. Once Somar was placed inside, he could be completely submerged.

Next to this was the "bath." A second inflatable vat, this one filled with water. The project to lay a water line from the river had made running water available to the whole colony, and Citadel's filtration system was still fully functional despite the damage to the tower. The water in the bath was pure and clear.

"I wonder if it would be better if it wasn't filtered?" Thomas asked.

Michaels and the assistant looked at him like he was crazy.

"You know — because Somar's people are plant-based. Maybe he could use the nutrients or something."

Michaels shook his head. "Maybe so, but I have a tough time ignoring forty years of medical practice just to stick an injured patient into a vat of dirty river water," he said. "Besides, the water comes to us filtered. Bringing unfiltered water would take time and manpower we don't have."

Thomas nodded. Michaels was right, of course. Thomas, ever trying to think ahead and plan for contingencies, was overthinking the water.

What else might he be overthinking?

I'm just worried, he thought. This entire exercise could prove futile. They could lose Somar, despite their efforts, and the choice Thomas had made would turn out to be for nothing. Two men might die today, and it would be his responsibility. His fault.

Michaels nodded to his assistant, and the two of them rolled the stretcher, moving Somar closer to the first vat. Michaels looked at Thomas. "Last chance to change our minds," he said.

Thomas inhaled, a deep breath that did nothing to relax him. "Is there any possibility of re-using the blood, after Somar is healed?"

Michaels shook his head. "I don't believe so. Based on what I've encountered in our database, the blood works until it doesn't. It contains some sort of semi-intelligent — well ... I'm not sure what to call them. Antibodies? Parasites, maybe."

"Parasites?"

"Not all parasites are bad. Humans have a number of parasites living in our bodies. Some perform vital functions that help keep us healthy and alive. The Esool have one that seeks out damaged cells and repairs them. It seems to be able to read some sort of cell memory. Earth Colony Fleet is studying Esool blood like crazy, trying to synthesize it."

Thomas rolled his eyes. "Of course they are."

Michaels gave him a knowing look, then turned back to the pod.

"Once the blood has taken effect we'll move him to the water. I'm not sure if this part's necessary, but I know that hydration helps him heal, so I think it's worth the effort."

Thomas took up a spot next to Michaels and the assistant. "I'll help," he said.

Michaels nodded, and then counted to three before all three men lifted Somar up and over the lip and into the vat of blood. In an instant he sank out of sight, and Thomas found himself holding his breath.

The blood had the sort of syrupy, viscous look that Thomas would have expected, but had the saving grace of being tinged green. He wasn't sure he could stomached this if the blood had been red.

So much blood — enough to fill an inflatable vat and cover a man head to toe. How long had Somar worked on this, feeling the pain of a needle each day, sacrificing his personal strength and energy? Would he have done it, if he'd known he would not save Alonzo after all? Would he have done all this if he'd known he'd save only himself?

They waited several seconds, closing in on a full minute, and nothing seemed to happen. The blood was calm and glassy now, too opaque to see through. Thomas looked at Michaels, staring at the vat. He was about to ask the doctor what they should do next, when the surface of the blood broke, and Somar rose, gasping.

"What has happened?" he managed, before slipping on the vat's edge and falling back into the blood.

As Thomas watched, the blood changed color, shifting from a healthy and natural-looking green to a faded brown, like the color of dried leaves. It seemed to shrink and compress, to collapse inward a bit, as if it were decaying right before their eyes.

Michaels and his assistant were already reaching into the vat when Thomas came to his senses, reaching in beside them, taking Somar by the arms and hoisting him up and out of one vat and into the other. Again, Somar sunk below the surface. Thomas watched as tiny eddies of brownish blood swirled from Somar's body, forming dense little clouds all round, eventually blocking him from view.

Minutes passed, and again Thomas worried. Had they

drowned him? Was this all wrong? What did they know about Esool physiology?

But Somar again broke the surface, rising from the water and standing on his own two feet. He needed no assistance. He was as strong and healthy as he ever was.

Thomas couldn't help himself. He smiled, and felt a tear roll down his cheek. "Somar," he said.

Somar looked at him. "Thomas," he replied. "You have used my blood to heal me."

Thomas nodded, unsure whether Somar would approve or become angry.

As he watched, Somar nodded his head, sighed deeply, and then looked up at all three of the humans. *"Even our plans belong to life, and life laughs with delight in them,'"* Somar intoned.

All were quiet for a moment, until Thomas said, *"Man plans, God laughs."*

Somar's eyebrows arched in surprise, and then he nodded. "Wisdom comes in many forms, it seems. The *Book of Nolad* is but one."

"You feeling ok?" Michaels asked. "Are you fully recovered?"

"I am, Doctor. Thank you."

"Then you may want to get dressed," Thomas said. "There's a colony out there that needs you. Now more than ever."

CHAPTER 4

ADMIRAL NORCHEK PREFERRED TO CALMLY ASSESS EVERY
situation, to determine the best solution based on the facts
and resources at hand. In working with the humans,
however, he had come to realize that not all of the available
information and resources were available to him. After
many long conversations that went seemingly nowhere,
Norchek could only conclude that humans preferred to
keep all information secret until it was absolutely necessary
to reveal what they knew.

This was a dangerous game. Norchek felt that the
secrecy was a hindrance to progress, and may have jeopardized the mission.

Admiral Salazar, of the human Earth Colony Fleet, was
leading yet another meeting to discuss data received from
the lightrail network. "Once they left this hub, designated
Epsilon 30-A, they appear to have changed direction. This
was the point at which they would leave the established
lightrail network and rely on their own relays."

"Admiral Salazar," Norchek said, interrupting in a way
that was most uncharacteristic, and which alarmed the

other Esool officers in the room. "We reviewed this data yesterday. Has there been a new development?"

Salazar looked at Norchek for a long moment. Norchek had spent enough time with humans to recognize the expression — distaste and anger over a slight to the man's authority. Any other time, Norchek might apologize for giving offense. Not this time.

"Admiral Norchek, we know that you, of all people, have a more ... *personal* stake in finding this colony vessel."

Norchek nodded. "Indeed. Captain Somar was onboard on my orders. I have a responsibility to his line to determine what has become of him. Beyond that, there are many souls aboard that vessel, and the longer it takes to find them the more danger they may face."

"Everyone in the room is aware of that fact, Admiral," Salazar said, his jaw clenched and his face reddening. It was a peculiar trait of humans, this ability to "blush." It gave away so much about their emotional state. Humans practically broadcast their emotions with every bit of their physiology. It was as if the humans were deluged in data, to the point of being blind to it most of the time. Perhaps that was why they chose to keep so many secrets. Any bit of information they could actually control would be precious indeed.

"Why do we persist in reviewing data that is already known? Do we have vessels searching the area of their last known location? Have we determined their altered trajectory, after leaving Epsilon 30-A?"

Salazar looked as if he were about to reply, but instead sighed, his shoulders drooping as he relaxed. "No, Admiral. We haven't been able to determine anything. The truth is, we have no idea what happened. Whoever altered their course did a remarkable job of covering his tracks. This seems to have been planned for some time. We have uncovered a data trail leading back at least a year."

Norcheck's eyes widened. "This is new information."

"It's irrelevant," Salazar said, waving it off.

"I disagree. I would very much like to have access to this data trail. If my people could analyze ..."

"It's classified," Salazar snapped. He turned back to the display where he'd been pointing out redundant and useless information, and seemed to think better of continuing the charade. He turned again to the room. "I will have my people inform all of you if there is any change." He turned and left without another word.

Those who remained, both Esool and human, looked at each other blankly for a moment, and then all eyes fell on Norchek, who stood and walked to the display. His access was limited, but he had enough system authority to reach out and swipe the display, wiping it blank. He turned to the room, and addressed the remaining Esool, ignoring the humans. "This represents everything we currently know." And with that he left the room.

It was a shamefully dramatic display, and he regretted it as soon as he'd reached the corridor. But the feeling passed as he considered the truth of his words. They really did know nothing at all. Or, that is to say, the *Esool* knew nothing. Despite the vaunted proclamations of leadership within Earth Colony Fleet, the Human-Esool Exchange was not the peace-building arrangement it was meant to be. Somar — his friend and subordinate, and the first of the Esool to join a human colony — was lost. The entire program was in jeopardy, thanks to racial tensions from members of the ECF. The very peace between the Esool and the Humans could falter because of this.

It was never on stable ground to begin with. The Esool

had bent and compromised to the point of absurdity to broker the peace, surrendering their own lightrail network and becoming willfully dependent on the humans for faster-than-light travel. It had been necessary, the Esool leadership believed. Norchek himself had agreed that it was better to compromise than to continue a long and brutal war.

And now, despite all they had sacrificed to build peace with the humans, it could all crumble to dust.

Norchek needed more information. He needed to know more about that data trail, and more about how the lightrail network had been compromised. If this investigation was to make any headway, Norchek had to have a source of information he could trust.

During his time among the humans, he had encountered many surprising individuals. None more so than Joshua Foster.

Foster was a mid-ranking non-com officer in the ECF, and his duties seemed to primarily consist of running errands. "If there's ever anything you need, you let me know. I can get it. Doesn't matter how … *unusual*. And I'm very discreet, so ask me for anything."

Norchek had at first dismissed this, but over time realized that Foster was very well connected. Norchek had observed certain "arrangements" that Foster made for some of the human officers, for contraband of every description. More than once, Norchek had seen Foster escorting a young human female into the Officer's Quarters. Many such young females had come and gone during Norchek's time on Earth.

Foster was easy to find in the human facility. There were numerous ECF officers performing various tasks, coming and going, but Foster could often be found in a small office on one of the sub floors. He played loud music as he worked, using one of the handheld devices that all humans carried and used obsessively.

When Norchek entered the office, Foster glanced up, made a quick gesture with one hand, and the music stopped. Norchek suspected that whatever information had been on the display of Foster's handheld had also disappeared with that gesture.

"Admiral Norchek," Foster said, smiling. He was one of the few humans who seemed to genuinely like working with the Esool. Perhaps it was because the Esool were unconcerned with his side business.

"Mr. Foster," Norchek nodded in greeting. "Would you have a moment to speak with me?"

Foster's smile broadened, and he made another gesture, which caused the door to close behind Norchek.

"This feels like a private conversation," Foster said.

"Indeed."

"What can I do for you, Admiral?"

Norchek looked around the room. "Are you certain there are no recording devices here?"

Foster laughed. "There are *absolutely* recording devices here, but I control all of them. It doesn't matter, though, because I have a continuous recording going anyway. You can never be too careful. Plus, information is sort of one of my trades, so it's good to have a steady supply."

Norchek considered this, and decided his need was greater than his caution. "That is, in fact, why I am here. I wish to employ your services."

Foster squinted at him. "For information? You're an Admiral. Your access is going to be way higher than mine."

"Perhaps," Norchek said. "However, it has come to may

attention that not all information is being shared with my people. I need someone who can ... what is the phrase?"

"Fill in the gaps?" Foster offered.

"Yes. The gaps. There are many gaps."

"Sounds human. And military," Foster said. "What information do you need, exactly?"

Norchek explained his needs, specifically the need to backtrack data from the sabotage of Epsilon 30-A. "Beyond that, however, I have need of any information that pertains to the Citadel colony vessel."

"Wherever that information leads?" Foster asked, a note of caution in his voice.

"Let us begin with anything you can discover about the alterations to the lightrail hub, and go from there."

Foster nodded, smiling. "Now, about payment ..."

"I can provide currency, if that is your wish, but procuring it would bring unwanted attention," Norchek said. "Perhaps there is something you will accept instead?"

Foster thought about this. "I think there is. I've heard rumors." He made another gesture, and everything in the room dimmed. The main lights shut off and only a set of emergency lights remained active. Foster touched the lapel of his jacket and Norchek heard a small beep. "I've shut off every recording device in this room, and on my person. You're going to have to take my word for it."

Norchek nodded. "I have no choice but to trust your word."

"Good. Because like I said, I've heard rumors ... about Esool blood."

REILLY WAS PISSED OFF. She'd been a little groggy when she'd first awoken, and had been happy enough to drift and doze as medics checked her monitors and made sure she was comfortable. That willingness faded as she started feeling first rested and then restless.

Plus, there was a growing feeling of *too much*.

Too much fuss. Too much bother. Too much attention.Too much of everything except the one thing she couldn't get enough of.

Too little Mitch. Too little of her husband.

Husband, she thought, for the hundredth time, completely unable to keep the smile from her lips even despite her mood.

It still got her — still made her feel a tingle, and a twinge of nausea, and a lot of nervous excitement. She and Mitch ... *married*. She never saw that coming, back in those hectic days between cryo sleep on Captain Alonzo's ship. Mitch Garrison was all business and all duty back then, and she was a pilot who was technically lower in the hierarchy. They might have flirted, from time to time, but there wasn't much chance of getting together. Not with Mitch.

So with everything that had come of crashing on this world, Reilly now considered it a blessing. If not for coming here, she and Mitch would still be separated by miles of chain-of-command. She'd still be alone during those shifts between sleeping in stasis.

She'd had enough of sleep, especially in the past couple of days.

Now that she was awake, and could actually spend time with him, where was he? Off cleaning up messes, fixing things, *saving people.*

So typical.

She smiled.

She was irritated about all of the attention people were forcing on her, irritated that she was hurt, and irritated that

Mitch wasn't here. But she did love that guy, with all her heart, and she was never more proud of him than she was right now.

"You're looking better," she heard a voice say. She looked up to see Janet stepping closer and smiling down at her.

"If one more person tries to make me feel 'comfortable' I'm going to stab them," Reilly said.

"Definitely feeling better," Janet said.

Reilly managed to shake off some of her irritation, taking a deep breath to calm herself. "Where's Mitch? How's it going out there? Where's Mitch?"

"You asked that twice," Janet laughed.

"It's the part I care about most."

"Mitch is doing a great job. Things are really moving now, especially with all the levitating."

"Levitating?" Reilly asked.

Janet told her about the modified "repulsor crane" that was helping clear debris, making the rescue effort easier. She also told her about the strange boy who had floated out of the tower wreckage with Penny and Taggart in tow.

"Weird," Reilly said. "Did the boy modify the repulsor?"

Janet hesitated, and Reilly knew instantly who had done the work. "Alan," she said, her tone going cold.

"He was helping," Janet replied. "He helped a lot today. There are people who wouldn't be alive right now if it wasn't for him."

"There are a lot of people who *would* be alive, if it wasn't for him. Or wouldn't be injured in the first place, or might be *home* instead of ..." She hesitated. She was going to say *instead of stuck here*. But hadn't she already decided that being here had been one of the best things to ever happen to her? Was that selfish?

Janet nodded. What could she say? Reilly knew that it wasn't reasonable to pin everything on Alan.

Or maybe it was. He'd arranged for them to come to this world, hadn't he? There was that trick with the cancellation wave, wiping out the minds of the colonists. Wasn't it Alan that caused all of this in the first place?

But if he was helping ...

"Where is Mitch?" she asked. "Is he still busy?"

"Yeah, but I can get him," Janet said. "I know you want to see him, and he'd come running if he knew you were asking for him."

"No," Reilly said, looking around. None of the medics was paying attention. They all had more critical patients to deal with. Reilly quickly tugged the IV needle out of her hand, wincing a bit. She kicked the covers from her and stood, a bit unsteady at first. The monitors chimed, sensing that she was no longer in the bed. She quieted them with a few quick taps on the display.

"What are you doing?" Janet asked in a whisper.

"I'm going to him," she said.

"But you're hurt! You need to rest!"

"I'm rested. And I can walk, so how hurt can I be?" she asked, wincing suddenly from the pain in her ribs, but trying (unconvincingly) to play it off. "I can't lie here anymore. I have to get out and *do* something. It's therapy."

"I think Dr. Michaels would disagree."

"I certainly *would*," Reilly heard a stern voice say from behind her. She looked back to see Michaels glaring down. His arm was out of the sling now, but it dangled heavily at his side, weighed down by a somewhat dirty-looking arm cast, tinged light green.

"Doctor ..." Reilly started.

"Back in that bed. *Now*."

Reilly almost did it. Her chain-of-command instincts kicked in and she had just started to reach for the blankets, to slip in and cover herself, to do what she was told — but she hesitated. She nodded at the cast Michaels wore. "How long did you lay around when you got that?" she asked.

Michaels glanced down a the cast, then glared at her, and swore. He waved his good hand dismissively as he turned and walked away, grumbling about taking care of patients who weren't giving him guff.

"That was impressive," Janet said.

"That was piloting. I pretended he was a debris field and just punched it."

Janet laughed, and Reilly joined her, then winced as the pain stabbed her through the side.

"You're sure you're up for this?" Janet asked.

"No," Reilly said. "Now let's go find my husband."

"THANKS FOR BRINGING HIM," Alan said.

"What are you planning to do?" Penny asked, concerned. She felt somehow responsible for Edward. They had shared a mind, so in a way there was no one in the universe who could know him the way she did.

That wasn't saying much.

"I'm going to scan him, mostly. I have some readings from earlier, when the Current was in control of Mr. Meyers. I also have scans of Mr. Taggart and ..." He stopped abruptly.

"Your dad," Penny said, quietly.

Alan nodded.

Penny looked at Taggart, who was sitting on the edge of one of the exam tables, taking the weight off of his injured legs, which were distracting him from the conversation at hand. He glanced up at the mention of his name. "Anything I can do to help," he offered.

Penny was relieved, for some reason, that he hadn't picked up on Alan's hesitant mention of his father. She still wasn't *sure* about Taggart. He was so different from the man she knew — though she had to admit that most of her contact with him had been pretty formal. He was never one to soften, to be candid without some ulterior motive. But here he was, vulnerable, injured, but somehow humble.

It could be an act.

True, and she wouldn't put it past him. Taggart was certainly capable of keeping up appearances, behaving as if he were a changed man. She felt certain he could do that indefinitely, if he wanted.

But it just didn't feel right to her. It wasn't just what he said, or even how he acted. Taggart's whole demeanor had changed from the way she remembered him. His body language, the way he held himself and the expressions on his face, all the subtle and silent clues that gave an insight into who someone was and what they were thinking — all of the *nuance* of Taggart was different. The arrogance and swagger were gone, and in their place was a sort of ...

Peace, Penny thought. *He seems to be at peace with himself.*

"Would you mind asking him to move to the exam table?" Alan asked.

Penny looked from Taggart to Edward. The boy was floating serenely above the floor, his eyes fixed on some distant spot. Penny swore he must be seeing something beyond anything she could see. Something distant, or maybe in a different spectrum of light. His face had no real expression, but he, too, had a sort of unspoken language. Penny could tell from his demeanor, his focus on things beyond the room and the moment, that he was seeing something awe inspiring. Something *majestic*.

"Edward," she said quietly.

Without a word, and without shifting his gaze, Edward slowly floated to the exam table. And then he did the most remarkable thing ...

He sat.

Full contact, right on the table, and none of the things Penny had assumed would happen if he touched the ground. Not one spark, no burst of white light, no explosion. Just a boy sitting on an exam table.

"I was expecting fireworks," Penny said, smiling.

Edward finally looked at her, his expression still as unreadable as it had ever been. "I am containing my ambient field and preventing unwanted discharges."

"Not here, Edward," Taggart said from his own perch, smiling. "There are ladies present." He laughed, a sort of light-hearted chuckle that sounded a little self-deprecating, as if he wasn't sure if his own joke was funny. That was definitely a different Taggart than the one Penny knew. And because of that, she laughed a little along with him, to reassure him.

Speaking of people changing, she thought. *When did I become so ... concerned?*

Alan stepped closer to Edward and used one of the handhelds to take a scan. "You're very interesting," Alan said.

Penny and Taggart exchanged looks, and then both laughed out loud.

"I don't understand," Edward said.

"I don't think Alan does either," Penny said, smiling. She was looking at Alan, who seemed a little sheepish, but otherwise was as distant as he'd ever been. He had a light smile, a trace of "getting it" on his lips and in his eyes. That was when Penny realized.

He's changed, too. None of us are who we were.

Alan consulted the handheld. "According to the scans, Edward is an energy field. Sort of a floating electromagnetic bubble in a human shape." Alan showed the handheld to Taggart and Penny. She pretended to understand what she was seeing, but she was more interested in what she'd just learned about Edward.

"He's right about the ambient power. Not a trace of it. Earlier, when the Current was controlling Mr. Meyers, there was an EM field surrounding him, messing with all of the instruments. But Edward shows no signs of that."

"So what exactly is the 'Current?'" Penny asked. "I've heard that a couple of times.

Alan looked up from the display. "Yeah, you were ... out of the loop, I think. Yesterday a man walked into the colony, acting strange. He was being controlled by something that called itself the Current. From what I can tell, the Current is a being made of pure energy."

She looked at Edward. "You," she said.

"The many. We are many," Edward said. "I am Edward. We are the Current."

"There are more of you?" Taggart asked. "On this world? A population?"

Edward turned to look at him, though Penny thought that the motion might be for their benefit more than his. He seemed to see without the need for eyes. Eyes were a habit.

"We are here," Edward said.

Alan, Penny and Taggart exchanged looks. Finally Taggart asked, "Here, as in all of you? You're all here in this room?"

Edward didn't speak for a moment, and then, "It's hard to explain. I'm new. Different. The Current is here, in me."

Penny caught on. "It's you? You're all of the current? All wrapped up in one shape?"

"We are many who are one. We want to be many."

"And you have been absorbing the waveforms, from the pods," Alan said. "The many. You're ... oh my God ..."

Penny blinked. "What? What is it?"

Taggart stood and limped over to one of the displays near Edward. He tapped the screen a few times. The displays lit up, and what looked like thousands of brain patterns appeared on screen. They began to overlap and combine, and as they did so the scan of Edward lit up in areas, until much of the patterns corresponded and matched. "It's true," he said quietly. "Unbelievable."

Alan joined him at the display and Penny stood behind, trying to understand what she was seeing.

"What is it? What's happening?" she asked.

Alan turned to face her. "The waveforms. All of them. Edward's scan is like a mishmash of thousands of First Colony waveforms." He looked back at Edward, then said quietly, "I did this."

Taggart put a hand on his shoulder. "No, Alan. This was a side effect. Unintended. It's not your fault."

"How many lives can I ruin?" Alan said, and for the first time since Penny had known him he sounded *small*. He sounded like a child, vulnerable and alone and afraid.

"So Edward has all of the First Colony personalities in his mind?" she asked.

It was Taggart who answered. "The many. The Current has been absorbing waveforms, and those are manifesting as personalities. But they're locked together, unable to separate from the whole. The many who are one."

She looked back at Edward, who was unreadable at the moment. "But not you," she said.

"I was different."

"The autism," she said. She looked back to Alan and Taggart. "Edward was autistic."

"And he was joined with your mind," Alan said, quietly. "Also my fault." He shook his head. "When the Current encountered you, it must have tried to make contact, and Edward ... jumped. Or something. This is new territory."

They all turned back to Edward, who sat quiet and unmoving on the table.

"More than the Current expected?" Penny asked.

Alan stood beside her, and said quietly, "Humans, our technology, everything that I brought here — I think it was *all* more than the Current expected. I think I brought an infection here."

THERE ARE SO **many of them**, Edward thought as he looked around.

He wasn't using his eyes. Functionally, those were useless. Decorations. Symbols. Memories. His real vision was so much more than anything his human eyes could ever see.

He saw *everything* now.

He saw the humans of the colony — colored auras moving about, doing everyday tasks. He could see them even through the walls of the lab.

He could also see the life on this planet — every tree, every bird, every insect. He could see the invisible energy generated by wind and water as they moved over dry ground and through dry air.

Beyond the world, beyond the barrier of the atmosphere, he could see an expanse of universe stretching further than even his sight could explore. If he looked hard enough, he could see thin hints of the layers of reality, as if there were worlds and universes beyond this one.

And then there was the web of light. Spanning the infinite darkness of the universe, ranging from star to star as far as his new perception would let him see, there was the web of the lightrail network.

He knew what the lightrail was because Louis Angelou knew what it was — because Taggart had known what it was, and because Penny knew, on a high level, what it was. Even the man, Meyers, who had been host to the Current on a strange and shambling walk to the colony, had known what it was. And Reilly, the pilot whom the Current had spoken to. And the dozens of colonists the Current had ... the Current had ...

Killed.

Edward nearly moaned with grief. The Current had no concept of death. Not really. Only what it had learned from the transient waveforms it had absorbed, and the knowledge it had gleaned from brief encounters with human minds. It hadn't known, at the time, that it was causing such irreparable harm. It hadn't been aware of how unspeakable its actions were.

But Edward knew.

Better to think of the numbers. *All* the numbers. The number of displays in this room. The number of buildings in the colony. The number of small animals nearby. The number of humans on this world — separate and individual and living lives all their own.

Think of that.

Even with the memories of the waveforms, and experiences with humans such as Reilly and Meyers, the Current hadn't had much concept of numbers. But Edward did. Discovering Edward had changed everything, just as merging with Penny had changed everything for Edward.

Edward's waveform dominated the Current, shaping and controlling the energy as if it were his own body. Things were very different. They were *better*. Edward and the Current were one now. And they could see so much.

The lightrail was the most interesting thing they could see.

It stretched and wound its way among the stars — invisible to the humans, but shining like threads of golden light to Edward. The pattern stretched like a net throughout the galaxy. It spun into infinity, far beyond even Edward's newfound range of vision. And it called to him.

No ... it called to *them*. Despite Edward's dominance of the Current, they were still *the many*. The waveforms were growing stronger, each yearning for dominance, each wanting to live as an individual.

There were more waveforms, among the humans. He could see them. Edward could draw them out, pull them from their hosts as the Current had with Meyers. He could make them part of the many.

But should he? As yet, he hadn't been able to separate individual personalities. They were there, struggling to be autonomous, but something prevented it. Or perhaps something was missing.

By instinct, Edward knew that they could all be separate, living lives apart from the many, as individuals. He just hadn't worked out the *how*.

For the first time in his life (both lives — all *three* lives, really)Edward's autism had turned out to be a gift. When it came to understanding the waveforms in the minds of the colonists, he could see the patterns, how everything was tangled together. He believed that with enough time he could find a way to untangle them.

After being a part of Penny's mind for a time, Edward now had more tools for reasoning and understanding in ways that had been difficult for him before. He could look beyond the patterns now, and beyond the compulsions. With every personality he touched, he gained more insight.

So maybe he should absorb all of the First Colony waveforms. Maybe then he could see a clear way to untangle them, to make them individuals. Maybe that insight was worth the risk of adding more desperate souls to the many. More knowledge, more perspective, more instinct. If he absorbed all of the First Colony waveforms, the Current would grow. Its burden would grow as well, it was true. That risk might be worth it, if it meant understanding the problem better, coming to a solution faster.

And maybe then he could see about reaching out to the distant network of light and, someday, maybe even those layers beyond.

CHAPTER 5

MITCH HATED BEING PROUD OF ALAN'S WORK. BUT DAMMIT, he was. The repulsor crane was pure *genius* — a machine finely tuned to do delicate work on a large scale, yet cobbled together from spare parts and sweat and maybe a little wishful thinking. That was brilliant. That was *Alan*. The Alan that Mitch had known and cared about, before all this. Before the betrayal.

Given that betrayal, Mitch wondered, should they even be using this technology? Wasn't it a little like using a medical procedure perfected by torturers in a concentration camp? Was it unethical? Did the ends justify the means?

No. It didn't matter. This was one of those times when it was better to look past the source and go straight to the benefit. With the crane they were now clearing the last of the large debris. Mitch organized teams into shifts, allowing groups to rest and recoup while others worked on cannibalizing the debris for parts. There was still rebuilding and repair to be done, and they'd need everything they could salvage.

More of the same, Mitch thought. They'd danced this

dance for weeks now, pulling survival by the hair out of a pile of ash and wreckage. He felt the bitterness threaten to take over him again, and he bit it back as he looked at the wreckage of the Citadel tower.

For the most part, it still stood, tall and proud despite the damage and fire-blackened bits of conduit and metal that spiraled upward. It made the tower feel a bit more *imposing* than hopeful, but the fact that it remained standing at all was encouraging. It was as if the tower, still reaching up into the sky, still standing for everyone to see, was also still standing for the hope of everyone here.

Mitch wasn't the only one feeling this. He saw the others glancing at the tower from time to time. They were all covered in soot and dirt and blood (their own as much as anyone else's), and they were all quiet from exhaustion. But the quiet *felt* like reverence.

Mitch could sense a growing pride in the colonists. Where there had been a deep division, just weeks ago, between Blue Collars and White Collars and the wealthy class, now there were just *people*. Humans, doing what humans do — pulling together, surviving, working for the good of all. The occasional glances toward Citadel seemed, to Mitch, to be a quiet gratitude. Sips from the well, to give strength.

Or maybe he was just exhausted and delirious.

"You look like you've seen better days."

He turned to see Thomas and Somar walking toward him. Thomas was a little bandaged and bruised, but Somar looked ...

"You're in a lot better shape than the last time I saw you," Mitch said, shooting Thomas a quizzical look.

"Nothing a good bath couldn't cure," Thomas said, smiling, though it didn't look quite genuine.

"I am recovered enough to be of assistance, I believe," Somar said.

Mitch nodded, willing to let Somar and Thomas have their secrets. Why not? Thomas, despite being so genuine and open most of the time, was a man who had many secrets. Some of the biggest secrets Mitch had ever heard of, actually. And by now, Mitch knew — or at least chose to believe — that Thomas only kept secrets when they really mattered, when revealing the truth could cause more harm than good.

"Reports indicate that all of the injured colonists have been retrieved and are receiving medical care," Somar said.

"Yes," Mitch said. "The casualty rate is pretty high, Captain. A few hundred injured, and about 20 dead. Many of the injured are in critical condition."

Somar nodded, his expression grim.

Something wasn't quite right about him, Mitch thought. He seemed well enough, but he was somehow more *stoic* than usual. Thomas, too, seemed a little off.

"Is there something I need to know?" Mitch asked.

Thomas glanced at Somar, who was inspecting the remains of the Citadel tower. He then glanced at some of the engineers and workers nearby.

Mitch understood. "Maybe we can chat later. We still have a lot of work ahead. Now that the debris is cleared we're combing it for materials we can use in rebuilding." He nodded to Citadel. "The tower was damaged badly. Primary power is offline. One of the secondaries was completely destroyed. The other was on the far side of the tower and took minimal damage, but the power load of the entire colony is on it right now."

"How long will it last?" Somar asked.

Mitch shrugged. "I think it can go for a few days, at best.

I've already initiated power rationing procedures. Non-essentials are out. Medical is the priority. I've put the water system on a schedule, to pump fresh water in at set times each day. Filtration is still working."

"What of the shuttles? Might we use them for power for critical systems?"

"It can be done, yes. We have two working shuttles now. I'd like to keep one available for transport. There's still some debris at the colony module crash site. With the repulsor crane we might be able to salvage something that would be useful in repairing the tower."

Somar and Thomas looked to the repulsor.

"That's pretty cool," Thomas said. "I don't know if I would have thought of that," he looked up at Mitch, smiling. "You must be some kind of engineering genius," he said.

Mitch felt his face flush. "Alan," he said.

He could see Thomas struggle to keep the smile on his face. "Got it," he said.

"Mr. Angelou is quite capable," Somar said. "And, I believe, quite remorseful."

Thomas and Mitch looked to the Esool Captain. Mitch dreaded what was coming. He knew, deep down, what was about to happen.

So did Thomas, apparently.

"You're giving him a pardon?"

Somar nodded. "I am."

"Captain ..." Mitch started.

"Mitch," Thomas interrupted. "He knows. We *all* know. But no matter what Alan may have done, or how things turned out, this was never his intention." Thomas swept a hand in an arc, indicating the wreckage and debris, the soiled and dirty workers. "And he can help. He *is* helping."

"We can't trust him," Mitch said.

"Perhaps not," Somar said. "Perhaps, in the end, trust is not something that can be granted once and remain unchecked and untested. However, many have redeemed themselves in these past weeks. If this experience has taught us anything, has it not taught us that people are capable of change?"

Mitch looked around the colony. Blue Collars, White Collars, wealthy colonists — everyone was pitching in. A couple of weeks ago they were at each other's throats, about to go to war. Now, here they were, sweating and working together. Bleeding together. How could he deny that?

He saw Janet first, but just behind her was a face that made his heart skip. Suddenly the weariness of the past couple of days fell away, and he felt as light as the debris being lifted and moved by the repulsor crane.

Reilly, moving a little slowly but seeming otherwise ok, smiled when she saw him. It was infectious, and Mitch found himself smiling back as he rushed toward her. Before thinking it through he grabbed her in a big embrace. She made a small grunt, and he practically tossed her backwards in an attempt to stop hurting her.

"You ok? Did I hurt you? Shouldn't you be in bed? Where's Dr. Michaels?" This last he asked while looking around frantically.

Janet said, "She just stared the old man down like he was a cadet. I think he was scared of her. She should probably be in bed."

"I'm good, I'm good," Reilly laughed. And as if to prove it, she stood on her tip-toes and kissed Mitch on the fore-head, which was followed promptly by a kiss on the lips.

Mitch felt himself melt a bit. The exhaustion of the past few days seem to roll onto him as the tension of worry he'd felt for Reilly finally subsided. Now he could sleep. Now he could collapse into a bed, with her beside him, and sleep like nothing bad had ever happened. Maybe later he actually would.

"How's it going?" Reilly asked.

Mitch turned to glance back at Somar and Thomas. "There have been some unexpected turns, but otherwise good."

The three of them walked back to Somar and Thomas, and the entire group found a more or less private spot in the shade of the trees near the Citadel tower.

"We have much to discuss," Somar said. "It would be best to keep information tightly guarded."

Mitch glanced at Janet.

"That's my cue," Janet said, starting to leave.

"I should probably leave too," Reilly said.

"You should both stay," Thomas said. "You're both pilots, and you've both proven yourselves. We could use some out of the box thinking right about now, and I know Reilly is the expert there." He smiled, and Reilly smiled back.

"What's the agenda?" Mitch asked. "Rescue is pretty much wrapped up, and repairs are under way."

"We must now tend to long-term matters," Somar said. "I believe it is imperative that we find a means to re-establish contact with the lightrail."

Everyone was quiet for a moment.

"What would it take?" Thomas asked.

"Lightrail access," Mitch said. "Normally we would have an orbital platform to use as an anchor. The lightrail relays onboard could keep a tentative link to the lightrail and power it up whenever we needed to re-enter the network."

"We rescued some relays from the platform before it ... you know," Janet said.

"We have working shuttles," Reilly said. "I could take

one of the relays into orbit. They're designed to stabilize in space, right?"

"Yes, normally," Mitch said. "The problem is gravity. Those relays are usually dropped in open space, away from gravity wells. You'd practically have to leave the solar system to create a stable link. Not going to happen in a shuttle. If we had one of the exploratory probes in orbit, we'd be able to establish a link. Those are meant to stay stationary in geosync. But this planet never had a probe in orbit, so there's nothing up there. The relay will just fall into the atmosphere."

They stood, quiet and contemplating. "What about mounting a relay to the shuttle itself?" Thomas asked. "We don't need a permanent link, really. Not yet."

Mitch nodded. "Maybe. And with some fine tuning we could probably create a link. The problem is what to do with it once it's there. The shuttles aren't equipped to travel on the lightrail, and we have no probes or any other means of sending a message."

There was a long, sobering pause. Mitch felt helpless and irritated. He felt like he was just pouring water on the fire. But what could he do? It was true — with everything they'd been through, they just didn't have the resources they needed.

How could they be so close and come up short? After every miracle he'd seen over the past few weeks, how could they find themselves standing here with their options so limited?

"What about the Hidalgo?" Reilly said, suddenly. She was staring into the distance, as if daydreaming. She looked up to see everyone staring at her.

She looked at Mitch. "Remember? You and Captain Alonzo told me about it, on the platform. It's a 'back pocket' idea, right? Captains keep it in mind, in case they ever need it. If there was ever a time we needed it, I think it's now."

Mitch considered this, and shook his head. "That is ridiculously dangerous."

"What the heck is a Hidalgo?" Janet asked.

Mitch glanced from her to Somar and back again. "It's a Hail Mary," he said. "The Hidalgo was an ECF ship that took heavy damage during the war with the Esool. It was too damaged to survive a trip on the lightrail, but if they didn't get everyone out they'd all die. The Captain made the decision to attach lightrail relays to a shuttle and use them as makeshift lightrail engines. It damn near killed everyone onboard. Only one shuttle made it back safe."

"But they made it back," Reilly said, looking at him intently. "They had one shot, and it worked."

"With heavy casualties."

"I think we're not much better off, right?"

Thomas interrupted. "We are, actually. We're here. We're not in any danger of dying, as far as I know. We have this world, if not a connection to civilization. We could make a go of it here. Risk nothing and stay. That's an option."

They all looked at each other.

"Is that what we want?" Mitch asked.

"That is the pertinent question," Somar said. "I believe that our casualties demonstrate a need to re-establish contact. However, the risk of such may outweigh the benefits of remaining."

Mitch thought about this. They could make a go of it, here on this world. A separate offshoot of humanity, surviving outside the boundaries of human civilization. Many of them might die. Maybe all of them. Maybe soon.

But if there was a chance to return home, to get help, to maybe save everyone — Mitch couldn't see any choice.

"It's worth the risk for a small team," Mitch said. "A small group of us can go. If we don't make it, the colony goes on, doing its best. If we do, we can bring back help. Medical personnel and supplies, a new orbital platform, a way to get everyone home. We owe it to those who have fallen to give it a try. We owe it to everyone still alive. We haven't given up once since being here, and I'm not willing to do it now."

He turned then to Somar. "But it's not my call, Captain. What are your orders?"

Somar considered for a moment. "You are correct, Mr. Garrison," he said. "We have not given up. We will not. Start preparations."

———

"THESE ARE THE CODES," Rudford said onscreen, making a swiping motion on his handheld. The vehicle's built-in display changed slightly. A column of numbers appeared on the left-hand side of the dividing glass separating the Chairman from his driver. Along with the data there was a schematic and elevation drawing of the lightrail control system on Taggart Prime.

The arrogance of the man. As if having his name stamped on nearly every piece of equipment used by the colonies wasn't enough, he had to have a moon named for himself? The vanity was sickening.

Though, the Chairman had to admit, Taggart's system for instant communication between Earth and a colony world was an impressive feat. Taggart's technology could have changed the nature of the colonies forever, and perhaps he would have deserved a moon in his name at that. Still, it seemed a tacky measure, and the Chairman found Taggart's narcissism to be distasteful.

"When will the process be complete?" the Chairman asked.

"A few days," Rudford said. "O'Neill has been very cooperative. I haven't given him much choice."

"He is there with you?" the Chairman asked.

"Yes, sir. I haven't let him out of my sight, just as you ordered. I have surveillance on him at all times. He has ... unpleasant private habits."

"Yes, so his file has indicated. My apologies, dear Rudford, for both exposing you to this man's depravity and for sending you off world."

Rudford nodded. "It was necessary, though it will be good to return to Earth. I dislike lightrail travel. And the air on this moon tastes *metallic*."

"Artificial atmosphere, Rudford. Just as is used in the Tokyo ghettos. No matter. You will return in a few days and leave both O'Neill and that moon behind for good."

"Should I eliminate him now?" Rudford asked.

"I think not. If things do not go as planned, I would prefer to have him available to take responsibility. I assume the nanobot detonators are in place?"

"Yes, Mr. Chairman. There is a large cluster gathered near his *medulla oblongata*. Setting them off will instantly shut down his heart and respiratory system. Thanks to Taggart's communication technology we can detonate them from anywhere and at any time."

The Chairman smiled. "Rudford, I believe you are looking forward to a chance to use this technology."

"Yes, sir, it would bring me great pleasure. But only on your orders," he said, nodding in a slight bow.

The Chairman ended the call and settled back into the plush leather seats of the limousine. Soon it would touch down at his block of apartments in Golden.

He had always preferred being in the mountains while in stasis. Of course, these days the mountains were hollow, mined for every square inch of space possible and serving as housing and office space for millions. The Chairman's apartments were at the top of one of the mountains, the great Rockies that had once stood as a symbol of majesty in the old American days. His apartments housed an enormous staff, employed for everything from maintenance and cleaning to security and wet work.

The Chairman's personal quarters were a well-guarded secret. They appeared to be non-existent, depending on how you looked. The entrance was through a door that only revealed itself in the presence of the Chairman, or anyone the Chairman had designated as safe — Rudford was currently on that very short list. The doorway opened to a room that was never the same twice. Even if someone managed to get into it, they would be nowhere near the Chairman. The room was actually many rooms, rotating and moving through shafts and tunnels constantly shifting position. The Chairman could enter stasis on one mountain and awake several miles away.

Such was the level of personal security necessary to protect the true leader of Earth First.

Of course, to the world at large, the leader of Earth First was, in fact, Taggart. And indeed, Taggart had a great deal of influence within the organization. His word was law, for all practical purposes. Which was what made his betrayal even more of an affront.

The Chairman had been content to remain the "power" behind the Taggart throne, as each new generation of Taggart came to the position. The Taggarts were a useful front for the organization. Wealthy, charismatic, powerful — and each was given a regimen of training in business and practical work. Every Taggart youth was forced to earn his way to power, rather than have it simply handed to him.

This was noble, for certain. But it served another purpose. Each Taggart heir could be counted on to have deep roots among the working class — the Blue Collars. They would also have strong connections to the White Collars, though this was almost unimportant in the grand scheme. The Taggarts, as well as the Chairman, knew that it was the people who got their hands and faces dirty in service of the colonies that could turn the tide if things went wrong. The Taggarts were hedging their bets, building the framework for an army of loyalists, should the need arise.

The Chairman had allowed this for decades, because it fit nicely with the plans of the organization. Though the Blue Collars were the very souls who most often traveled away from Earth on colony vessels, they had no love for the colonies themselves. Nurtured properly, they would certainly be willing to turn on the whole system. In theory.

It was a theory worth keeping in mind. And as the Chairman considered Taggart's plan to co-opt the lightrail network for his own purposes, he realized that the Blue Collars would inevitably have played a large role. They would act as Taggart's army and enforcers on countless stranded vessels across the network. Their lives were tied to the lightrail — so controlling the Blue Collars meant controlling the lightrail completely. With the power to disable the network in one hand and the fierce loyalty of the Blue Collars in the other, Taggart would have unchallenged reign over all of the colonies.

Pity, his plans would come to nothing when the Chairman gave the order to dismantle the entire network for good.

As the limo settled onto the Chairman's personal

landing pad one of the footmen appeared from the house. He opened the limo door and assisted the Chairman in stepping from the vehicle. Because of his unusually large frame, and the weight that went with it, the Chairman had standing orders that his vehicle hover a full two feet higher from the ground than usual. This made it possible for the Chairman to turn in his seat and step down comfortably. Unfortunately for anyone riding with him, it was that much more awkward to make an exit. This was tolerable to the Chairman. Preferable, perhaps.

"Sir, welcome home. I have asked for your usual pre-stasis meal to be served at six o'clock."

"Thank you. I will have my meal on the East balcony this evening," the Chairman said. The footman nodded and scurried ahead to ensure that doors opened when they were meant to, that servants were absent from the corridors, that preparations were going as planned.

The Chairman entered and made his way to the study.

In most respects, this room was a mirror image of his offices in the Earth First headquarters. The Chairman preferred routine and consistency. He would have worked exclusively from his home, but felt that his presence in the offices helped keep a certain level of efficiency at play.

He took a seat behind his desk, and as the platform rose into position the display on his desk lit up with data. A call was waiting for him. Rare, but not unheard of. He tapped the screen to answer. "Speak," he said.

The image of DeCarte, one of the Chairman's informants in the headquarters of the Earth Colony Fleet, appeared onscreen. "Sir. I hope I am not disturbing you."

"No, DeCarte, you have caught me in a rare pleasant mood. Speak."

"There is still no news on the disappearance of the

Citadel colony vessel. There are a lot of brass here, though. Including some of the shrubs."

"Esool? At ECF headquarters? On Earth?"

DeCarte hesitated, then answered, "Yes, sir. They have been here for some time, as part of the Human-Esool Exchange. One in particular is pretty involved in the investigation. Admiral Norchek. He was part of the original negotiation to create the HEE program."

The Chairman felt his blood pressure rise, and then drift back to normal levels as the nanobots in his bloodstream made adjustments. They were half the reason he was still alive. Without them he felt certain he would have had a stroke years ago. The stress of his work was unbearable at times. There were far too many imbeciles in the Universe.

"Will the Esool be any trouble for us?" he asked.

"No, sir. Though Admiral Norchek keeps pushing for more info. The ECF brass have been withholding from him."

"But not from me, surely," the Chairman said.

"No, sir! No, I've gotten you all of the intelligence we have on the disappearance. I've attached it to this call."

The Chairman pulled up the file and examined it. "Not a great deal more than we knew before," he said.

"No, sir."

"You have been in contact with Rudford, correct?"

DeCarte noticeably blanched at the mention of Rudford, and the Chairman had to refrain from smiling. He dearly loved Rudford's reputation. It helped tremendously in keeping underlings in line.

"Yes, sir," DeCarte said. "He has engaged me and my men here at EFC as part of the preparatory work for seizing control of the lightrail."

The Chairman nodded. "He has informed you of the penalty for indiscretion, I am certain."

Again DeCarte paled and flinched slightly. "Yes, sir," he said, swallowing. "You can count on us, sir. We understand our orders and the need for secrecy."

"Very good. You will report to Rudford for the next few days. When I awake from stasis I expect to be able to shut down the lightrail network and end this nightmare once and for all. Do not disappoint me."

"No, sir, of course n—"

The Chairman abruptly ended the call and settled back in his chair.

The Esool— here on Earth. It disgusted him. This whole business of humans intermingling with the aliens, cavorting out among the stars, far from the home world — it was *repugnant*. Flipping the switch on the whole system couldn't happen soon enough, as far as he was concerned. Let space make a meal of all Esool and the traitorous human trash that mingled with them.

He started to reach for a butterscotch, but was dismayed to remember that the box was on his real desk, in his real office, several hundred miles away.

Ah, well, he thought. *Dinner will be served soon.*

"I don't trust him," Mitch said as he and Thomas neared the small structure that served as Alan's lab.

Thomas said nothing.

"Do you trust him?" Mitch asked.

Thomas looked at him for a moment, then shook his head, but said, "I'm not sure."

Mitch nodded. "You have history with him."

"In a manner of speaking," Thomas said. "He's the son of my best friend. To be honest, all of this is hard to adjust to. The last time I saw him, he was a kid. And he looked different. He's done some modification."

"It's what he does," Mitch said. He wasn't sure how much he should push Thomas on his level of trust with Alan. Since this began, Alan and Thomas had shared a sort of bond. It wasn't until things really started falling apart that Mitch discovered how deep that bond really went, and how far back in history. Thomas, destroyer of worlds.

But he wasn't, was he? No, that title now belonged to Alan. Everything Thomas had been accused of in his life, Alan had more or less done himself. Maybe not maliciously, maybe not intentionally, but the end result was the same, wasn't it?

"You ok with this?" Thomas asked.

"Are you? What happened, with you and Somar?"

"It's a long story. It's not something I want to go into right now."

"But you will?" Mitch asked. "Because, I have to tell ya, all the secrets — I think I'm getting past done with them. And you have more than anyone I know."

Thomas looked at him for a long moment, and for the first time since knowing him Mitch could see a sort of burden in his eyes. The laid-back and easy-going guy he'd been, the guy on his second chance, seemed distant now. This Thomas seemed burdened more than the "Destroyer of Worlds" had ever been.

But finding out the why of it would have to wait for another time.

They entered the lab and found Alan with Penny and Taggart. The boy, Edward, was sitting on an exam table.

Everyone looked up as they entered.

"Hope we're not interrupting," Mitch said.

"Not at all," Alan said.

Ice. That's all there was between them. But Mitch could sense it — Alan's desire to make things right, to sweep the past aside, to be forgiven.

He just … *couldn't.*

"You've been pardoned," Mitch said. Might as well get it over with.

Alan blinked, and his eyebrows went up. "Pardoned?"

"Somar," Thomas said. "He's making the announcement to everyone later, but everyone here can vouch for you. We already told your guards to go."

Alan nodded, but Penny and Taggart were all smiles.

Taggart clapped Alan on the shoulder, "Congratulations, son … Alan," he said, correcting awkwardly.

"Yeah, congrats!" Penny said, and hugged him, which seemed equally as awkward.

Pardoned, but not forgiven or forgotten, Mitch thought. *I guess I'm not the only one having a tough time with this.*

Alan nodded, and in an instant was back to his usual stoic self. "Good. Thank you. I'll do my best to live up to it."

Mitch said nothing.

"Turns out, we may have a chance for you to do that," Thomas said. He explained the Hidalgo plan, the risks, the challenges. Mitch listened to all of it while watching Alan closely.

"So we need to retrofit a shuttle with lightrail relays," Thomas said. "Do you think you can work out the logistics of that?"

Alan nodded. "It will be tricky. If we're off by even a small margin the relay could rip the shuttle apart the first time we initiate a lightrail connection." He looked to Mitch. "You are better with shuttle systems than I am," he said.

Mitch shook his head. "This is about more than mechanics or engineering. There's a level of science here I'm not qualified for. No one here is. Except you."

"And Uncle John ..." Alan said, then corrected. "Thomas. He was the head of the original lightrail project." He turned to face Thomas. "You can help me figure out the tolerances."

Thomas nodded. "Just promise not to call me 'Uncle John' again. There are already too many people around who know me for who I am."

Alan nodded.

Mitch wasn't sure that was entirely true. He was starting to wonder if he could know who *anyone* was these days. Anyone except Reilly, of course.

He also wasn't sure how to feel about all of this. Alan was stepping up, and they really did need him. But he was also trying so hard to make peace, to earn their trust again. Hadn't he done that for a year before this? Embedding himself in Blue Collar crews, learning to live, act, and think like one of them? Hadn't he managed to fool even Mitch, with this act of genuineness?

Taggart, stepping forward slightly and using one of the lab tables to support himself, said, "If the intention is to re-establish the lightrail, I may have a safer alternative than going home." Everyone in the room stared at him. He looked from face to face, "Maybe we can make a call."

THERE WERE **advantages to quietly watching.**

The Current had learned this as it had observed the humans all these weeks, moving invisibly within the colony and even onto the shuttle. Talking to humans directly had its benefits, but listening quietly could reveal so much more.

Edward knew this, too. All his life, people had a tendency to talk about him as if he were not in the room. His mother was always commenting that he was a sponge, that everything said in his presence would come up again, sooner or later. Though he didn't always understand what people were saying, he did hear much he *could* understand.

Now was different. Now he had the benefit of dozens of human minds within the Current, all thinking and processing as he listened. He had the benefit of his connection with Penny, who had taught him so much. He was different than before, but old habits lingered. He still had a tendency to sit quietly, looking off into the distance as he listened to the conversations of others, who chatted openly without even noticing he was there.

They were going to the lightrail.

This excited Edward, very much. His attention had never been more focused. Reaching the lightrail was the most important thing he could think of. It was all he wanted to do. It was exactly what he *would* do.

As everyone in the room discussed their plans, Edward paid close attention to every detail. Eventually, Taggart interjected with the news that he had a way to communicate using the lightrail, which excited everyone. Edward was interested in this, too, but soon after it was mentioned all of the men left to find Captain Somar. Edward found himself alone in the lab with Penny.

"Hey," she said, standing beside him. "How are you doing?"

Edward had always had a problem with direct eye contact, back in his human life. Now, as part of the Current, his eyes were more of an affect, part of the simulation of his body, generated by habit more than anything. They were, by and large, non-functional. He could "see" with every part of himself. But he was learning that it made Penny and the others more comfortable if he looked directly at them when they were having a conversation. He turned his head to face her. "I'm fine," he said.

"The others had to go talk to Somar. So I guess all the tests are over. We can leave, if you want. I don't really know where we could go, but I'm kind of tired of being in this lab."

Edward rose from the table — literally rising a few inches up and out as he lowered his legs toward the ground.

He noticed Penny flinch.

"I'm sorry. It must be strange to see me levitate."

She shook her head at first, then changed to a nod. "Yes. Yes it is. But that's just part of who you are. I'm fine. And I'll get used to it. I just want to know you're ok."

"Yes," he said. "I'm still ok."

She smiled and laughed a little. "Good. I'm sorry, I guess I just worry."

"Like my mother,"Edward said.

"Yeah, I guess so. Sort of like that."

"It's fine. I like it."

Penny gave him a strange look. "You're sounding a little different all of a sudden. More ..."

"Human?" Edward asked.

"Well, yeah, actually. Sorry. You *are* human, so that's kind of rude I guess."

"No, it's not. I'm not human. Not really. I'm the Current. And Edward. It's confusing, I know."

"A little," Penny agreed. "So, Edward 'Current' Ballar, now that you're free from tests for a while, what would you like to do?"

Edward did not have muscles. His features, as realistic as they may have seemed, were an illusion. But he remembered certain movements, and how they felt. He had not fully understood his emotions or the emotions of others, before all this began, and the Current had no understanding at all. But the more time he spent with Penny and other humans, the more he came to realize how much they *needed* emotions. They needed to see small movements of muscles, a crinkle around the eyes, a drawing of the lips.

Edward smiled. "I want to see *everything*."

CHAPTER 6

HE HAD TO BLAME IT ON HIS OLD SELF. WHICH MEANT admitting that he had a "new" self. And that was a tough thing for Taggart to admit, because in the end he really was a pompous and arrogant ass — *before*.

Now ...?

To say things had changed seemed so bizarrely understated that it made him want to laugh out loud. Given the circumstances, that wouldn't work in his favor.

Something happened when the Current touched his mind, back in the lab. The memories were hazy, but the longer he dwelt on it the more they came to the surface. One instant he had been Louis Alan, father of John Thomas Alan — who was calling himself "Alan Angelou" these days. The next instant he was Taggart again, blinking in confusion about his surroundings, about what he'd been saying, what he'd been *thinking* a moment before.

In the time since, Taggart had plenty of opportunity to think through what happened, and what was *still* happening. His memories, from the time that Louis had been running things in his head, were starting to become clear. It was like remembering a dream. As he moved around the colony, as he had conversations with others, a flash of *deja vu* would hit him. He'd remember a snatch of conversation between Louis and Alan. He'd recall something Louis wanted to keep in mind for later. He'd realize that he was using a phrase Louis liked to use, or making a joke where Louis would have made one.

Louis was still with him.

Whatever the Current had done to absorb the waveforms from the sleeping colonists, and from Meyers, it had not absorbed the waveform of Louis Alan. Instead, somehow, it had integrated it with Taggart's own mind more fully, more completely. Enough so that Taggart was no longer the man he'd been, but was someone new. He was some sort of amalgam of Taggart and Louis.

He wasn't sure how the others would react to this. It might make his knowledge and assertions suspect at a time when, he knew, they all needed to trust him. So he kept a lid on it, and secretly wondered at his new self, and his new desire to work for the cause of right rather than for the cause of Taggart.

But that old self, that was definitely to blame for not bringing this up sooner. "I have a way to communicate with the colonies," he said to the room.

Somar, Thomas, Mitch, Alan — four men whom Taggart had come to know and respect over the past few weeks. Or had he? A lot of what he knew and what he was feeling came from that other part of his mind, the Louis part. Alan's father.

"You mentioned this before," Somar said, "soon after you were recovered from the crash site. Intwined particles."

"Yes," Taggart said. "That's it."

"Entwined?" Alan said. "Do you mean *entangled*? Entangled quantum particles?"

Taggart looked at Alan and couldn't help the emotion that came over him. Something strange and new, which he had never felt when he was his old self. Not really. Not legitimately.

Pride. He was proud of his son.

Not my son, he thought, but it was a mournful thought.

"I think that's it. Entangled, yes. I know the protocols for linking communications with my system on ..." He paused, suddenly embarrassed.

"On what?" Thomas asked.

"I ... ok, I'm going to just get this over with. I can establish contact with Taggart Prime."

"Your moon," Thomas said, smiling. "I remember."

Taggart felt his face flush. "It was a different time." Everyone in the room seemed to smirk, and Taggart carried on. "I was given instructions for creating a link. My team discovered a way to do this through something they call 'sympathetic particles.' It requires Taggart Industries technology, of course. Proprietary."

"But since TI equipment is pretty standard everywhere, that's not much of a limitation, is it?" Mitch asked.

Taggart shook his head. "Not really, no. But the good news for us is that once I activate the system we will be able to communicate with anyone in the colonies."

"Fantastic!" Thomas said. "That might keep us from killing ourselves by strapping a lightrail relay to our backs!"

"We'll still need the lightrail, of course," Taggart said. "The whole system is dependent on it. That's how I was ..."

He stopped. This was a line he hadn't yet crossed, and once he had there would be no turning back. This was where he steeped away from his old self and embraced this new self, completely, wholeheartedly.

He took a deep breath. They were all staring at him, expectantly. "That's how I was planning to take control of the lightrail network."

There was silence in the room. "You're not planning to do that anymore?" Thomas asked.

"No," Taggart said, smiling. "It seems less like a good idea now."

"You told us of this plan, of course," Somar said. "But I assume something has changed. You're now willing to share the details?"

Taggart nodded "Yes. Absolutely. Because it could save everyone. That's the most important thing."

Again they were quiet, looking at each other. Mitch was the one who broke the silence. "Why should we trust you?"

Taggart didn't have an answer for that. Or rather, not an answer that would do any good. "You shouldn't," he said. "You absolutely should not. Because before yesterday, I was not someone who should be trusted. But then things ... changed."

"I'll say," Thomas smiled.

"But that's the point, Taggart," Mitch said. "You are who you are, and you've done what you've done."

"And now I'm offering to help."

Mitch nodded. "Ok. I can accept that. I can't trust that you don't have an ulterior motive, though. So you'll pardon me if I don't let you anywhere near that shuttle."

Taggart nodded. "Fair enough. I understand. I can turn over the codes, jot down the whole procedure. I don't have to be there for it to work. But I hope you'll see fit to give me a chance to redeem myself, someday."

"Mr. Taggart," Somar said, "our ordeal on this world has proven time and again that redemption is always possible."

"Here, here," Thomas said, holding up an imaginary champagne flute. Everyone chuckled. Even Mitch.

"Ok," Taggart said. "Let's get to work. Give me a hand-held and I'll start pulling together everything I know."

"REDEMPTION IS ALWAYS POSSIBLE." Alan heard the words, but wasn't sure he believed it.

A lot of people on this world had been able to redeem themselves, it was true. Uncle John, for certain. Taggart, perhaps. The Blue Collars who participated in the mutiny. Everyone had their sins to atone for. But ultimately, who really was the bad guy here?

I am, Alan thought. *I'm the bad guy after all.*

Somar had pardoned him, but it was clear that Mitch would never trust him again. Not as he had before.

Alan hadn't even realized how much he valued Mitch's trust. In the absence of his real father, Mitch had become a sort of surrogate. Betraying him to bring back the souls of First Colony had destroyed everything they shared.

And in the end, what had he gained for all his machinations and line crossing? Hundreds dead. Thousands stranded on an increasingly dangerous world. A new species infected by something *he* created. And his father ...

Taggart was already covering details of the quantum entanglement with everyone, but Alan was only half listening. Instead he was studying the man to see any evidence, any *trace* of his father still being there.

Taggart had changed, for certain. He had a demeanor that was very much like Alan's father. Quiet, compassionate, willing to help when he was needed. It seemed that being merged with Louis Alan had made Taggart a better man.

Or had it?

Who could determine that, objectively? Wasn't it a matter of perspective? Taggart was arrogant and self-centered, egomaniacal and bent on ruling humanity through manipulating the only means of faster-than-light travel that existed. Did that make him evil?

Was Napoleon evil? Alexander? Caesar?

These were men who bloodied their hands to build great empires. History might read them as evil, but history existed *because* of men like these. Was Taggart like them? And if so, what was Alan to Taggart's story? Or to the story of humanity?

Redemption might be possible for everyone, but not everyone deserved it. Being pardoned by Somar and the others wasn't redemption. His crimes still stood. Until he made things right, he might earn the forgiveness of everyone else, might even earn the trust of everyone again — but he would never earn those things from himself.

Taggart finished his explanations and handed over the handheld with all of the codes and procedures detailed and outlined. Mitch looked it over, nodding as he read, then looked up at Alan. "Take a look at this?"

Alan felt a strange thrill at the question. It wasn't wholesale forgiveness, but for the first time since this started he didn't hear a note of bitterness or anger in Mitch's voice. He took the tablet and looked over the protocols.

"This should be simple enough to execute, once we've established a connection to the lightrail. I can start making modifications to the shuttle's comms while I'm working on the Hidalgo retrofit."

Mitch nodded. "I'll be behind you, checking everything you do."

Blunt, but Alan could understand why. He nodded. "I'll run everything through you and Thomas."

"I'll also have an engineer with you at all times," Mitch said.

Again Alan nodded.

"Mitch," Thomas started ...

"At all times," Mitch said, and then left the room.

Everyone was silent for a moment, until Thomas said, "Alan, don't take it personally, Mitch is just ..."

"It's personal," Alan said, and looked from the door Mitch had just used to meet the gaze of everyone in the room. "It should be personal for all of you. Don't trust me. I haven't earned it." And with that he also left the room.

He was halfway back to his lab when Taggart caught up to him, hobbling painfully and using a makeshift cane. "Alan! Wait up, I'm not exactly running sprints at the moment." He chuckled as Alan stopped and turned to face him. He was still smiling amicably as he limped closer. "Are you alright?" he asked.

It was so genial, so *comfortable*, that for a second Alan forgot that his father wasn't still dominant. It felt so personal. Alan started to speak, but the words caught in his throat and he had to start over. "Yes, I'm fine. I'm just realistic. I don't deserve their trust now."

"True," Taggart said, nodding. "Neither do I. I don't deserve yours either, for that matter. I ... I know that this must be very difficult for you."

There was an unspoken word there, at the end. Taggart didn't say what Louis Alan would have said, but it hovered right on the edge. *Son.*

Maybe it was a habit now, something hard-wired into

Taggart's brain, like this new demeanor. Or maybe part of his father's waveform still lingered, still had some influence. Maybe, like Taggart's communication system on Taggart Prime, there was some kind of sympathetic particle at work ...

Alan's eyes widened, and Taggart looked at him curiously. "What is it? What's happened?"

"Nothing," Alan said, shaking his head. "It may be nothing. I'm not sure, really. But I think I have an idea about how to fix at least one problem I created, maybe two."

Taggart smiled and laughed a little. "There's problem solving to be done? You should have said so! How can I help?"

Alan gestured and Taggart followed him to the lab. "You already have, actually. Your comm system may help break through something I've had a very hard time trying to crack."

Taggart thought about this as they entered the lab and he limped to one of the tables, leaning against it, bending to rub his sore legs. "You're talking about the waveforms?"

"Yes. I was studying this from all angles before, but lost track of it when the tower exploded."

"Life is full of little distractions, right?" Taggart smiled.

Alan nodded, a little disturbed at how much Taggart sounded like his father with that joke. He shook it off. "Before, when we ran the Rorschach test, I found a way to identify the individual waveforms. I was really hoping I could use that to somehow pull them apart, to separate them. But they're so integrated with the colonists, and the link is becoming stronger each day. There's a short window for restoring the colonists to normal, and it's closing."

"And how does my comm system change that?" Taggart asked.

"Sympathetic particles. Quantum entanglement. It means that two particles are linked, so that whatever happens to one happens to the other. This link is bizarre. Einstein labeled this kind of thing 'spooky action at a distance.' It's always been hypothetically possible to link two quantum particles and use them as a means of communication. No matter how far apart they are, each particle would react to whatever stimulus the other is exposed to. So, for example, you could get a bunch of particles entangled with each other and write a computer program that reads the state of each in a binary pattern, the same way computers read data anyway. Basically, you can write a communication program that uses entangled particles to translate audio and video in two very remote locations.

"Your system does something pretty impressive. It establishes a sympathetic link between two quantum particles that have never had contact with each other."

"I never quite understood the science of it," Taggart admitted. "But that's essentially how my team explained it. The protocols I've outlined in that handheld are used to make a local particle become sympathetic with a remote particle, in another Taggart Industries comm system. Once they developed the technology I had it installed in everything. It's invisible, and takes no resources when it isn't in use. My plan was to take control of the lightrail network and then demonstrate to the colonies that I had solved the problem of instant communication. I would own the entire network."

Alan marveled at how openly Taggart could discuss this plan, which was technically treason. He was as frank about it as anyone could be. Completely unconcerned with any potential consequences of his past.

"How do you do that?" Alan asked.

Taggart looked confused. "Do what?"

Alan wasn't sure. There was *something*, some small feat that Taggart had accomplished and that Alan was still struggling with. Finally, after a pause, Alan knew what it was. "How do you forgive yourself?" he asked. "How do you move on from your past, the things you were planning, like they no longer have a hold on you?"

Taggart gave a light smile that hinted at a deep pain within. "I don't, Alan. I don't forgive myself. Not entirely. I accept myself, that's all. I accept that I was who I was, and now I am who I am."

"Sounds like forgiveness to me," Alan said quietly.

Taggart shrugged. "Maybe it is. But I'm not sure it's even necessary to forgive myself, when I'm no longer the man who did those things. Now I'm a man trying to earn the trust of others — trying to be *worthy* of that trust. You'll do the same, because in the end you are not the villain you think you are. You're a man who made some mistakes, when he was the man he used to be. Now you should just concentrate on being the man you are."

There was silence for a long while. Finally, Alan nodded.

Maybe. Maybe he could do what Taggart was doing, and move on from who he was when he made all of his bad decisions, all of his big mistakes. But to do that, he had to start making more of a difference. He had to correct those mistakes, as best he could.

He turned to one of the displays and began writing a piece of code. It was unique, and it built on what Taggart's team had created. It used the data from his scans of the colonists, of his father, of Taggart after the change. But most importantly, it used every scrap of data he had on the Current. "Edward is the key to this," Alan said. "This simulation should prove me right. If not, I don't know what else I can do." He finished and started the simulation. "It's going to be a while before this shows any results. In the meantime, I need to start work on the Hidalgo modifications." He hesitated, then said, "Would you like to keep me company? Me and whichever engineer Mitch has babysitting me?"

Taggart laughed. "I would, actually," he said.

They left the simulation to run, and as they walked from the lab Alan had the sudden feeling that, for the first time since this all began, his father was closer to him than he'd been in years.

"His name is DeCarte," Foster said. "He's always been a huge pain, but lately he's been turning up in places he shouldn't. He has people inside the ECF headquarters, listening in on practically everything. We're sort of ... rivals."

"He is gathering intelligence?" Norchek asked. "For whom?"

"Someone high up in Earth First."

"I have heard of this organization," Norchek said. "They wish to end colonization and isolate the population of Earth."

"Yeah, which is insane, but they've managed to turn it into a business model. Plus, it's kind of a cult, I think. They recruit celebrities to be their public faces, like that Corey guy. The vid star. Turns out he was onboard the Citadel colony ship."

"Earth First placed him on a colony vessel?"

Foster shook his head. "I think he went off the rails."

Norchek was not sure what Foster meant by this expression.

"Went rogue," Foster said. "I think he had his own

agenda, and I don't think Earth First was too happy about it. They have DeCarte digging for every scrap of information they can get about that ship, including the data trail leading up to the modifications to Epsilon 30-A. Sound familiar?"

"Do their interests coincide with my own? Perhaps we could form an alliance of a sort, to share information."

Foster shook his head. "Not even close. From what I can gather, they have something big brewing, and it has something to do with Taggart's moon."

"Taggart Prime," Norchek said. "Your report on this was very interesting."

"That's one word for it."

"Are there further details? Do we know what Taggart was planning?"

Foster shrugged. "Whatever it was, it wasn't good. He's dug up dirt on everyone involved in manufacturing or maintaining the lightrail hubs. Taggart Industries more or less owns the network, considering how much of their technology is integrated with it. Over the past few decades his family has done everything it could to own small pieces until they could own the whole thing. Some parts may not have the TI stamp on them, but you can bet Taggart owns a piece of every manufacturer."

Norchek thought about this for a moment. "And what of Earth First?"

"Taggart has ties to it. He's the public leader, actually. Which everyone always thought was ironic. Or silly. It's one of the reasons no one has taken Earth First too seriously. They're a bunch of propagandists, mostly. But they have power. *Real* power. They control a lot of money, and they use their network of celebrities and business owners to influence policies throughout the colonies. They've recently started taking a lot of interest in Taggart Prime.

They even sent this guy, Rudford, to oversee something there."

"Is Rudford highly placed in the organization?"

"He either is, or he works for someone who is." Foster paused now, and looked away. When he turned back Norchek could see that his expression was serious, pained. "Listen, I have to tell you, this Rudford guy is scary. There are rumors about him everywhere. When he turns up, it's usually not good. In fact, it's usually the first sign of the apocalypse. The fact that Earth First sent him off world is something all of us should be scared about."

"How is ECF leadership responding?"

"They're turning away and whistling in the dark. I think he may have something on half of them, thanks to DeCarte."

Norchek thought about this. "Earth First has taken an interest in Taggart Prime, and Taggart Industries has gained a full grasp of the lightrail network, through direct holdings and subsidiaries. Is this correct?"

Foster nodded. "That seems to be the gist of it."

"It seems clear that Earth First intends to seize control of the lightrail network. We must find a way to prevent this."

"I'll say," Foster said. "If they do something to the network, you'll definitely never see your friend Somar again."

"This is far greater than the loss of Somar, or even the thousands of colonists on that vessel. The Esool have dismantled their own lightrail network, as part of the peace treaty with Earth. I believe this man, Taggart, intended to to isolate the Esool. It would take centuries for us to rebuild, and in that time Earth's military would have distinct advantage. At this time, however, I believe that Taggart's plan is no longer one we should worry over. Given their agenda, Earth

First would simply shut down the network entirely, ending space travel for both races."

Foster said nothing, but only nodded.

Norchek made a note on his handheld, a reminder to look deeper into Earth First and its leadership. He then set the handheld aside and reached into the bottom drawer of the small desk in his quarters. He removed a package wrapped in plain paper, and handed it to Foster.

"Thank you," Foster said.

"How is your daughter?" Norchek asked.

Foster smiled, though it had a touch of sadness. "She's doing much better. Better than I've seen her. I think it's working."

"I am pleased," Norchek said, nodding his head slightly.

Foster stood and prepared to leave, but turned back and said, "Admiral, I know we have an arrangement, and this is the payment. But I can't tell you how much I appreciate this. My ex and I … we don't get along. But my daughter means everything to me. I hardly get to see her. And since she's been sick, it's been more difficult. You're giving me a chance to spend time with her, to see her get better. Thank you."

Norchek nodded again, respectfully, and Foster left, closing the door behind him.

Alone, Norchek considered what he'd learned. Earth First was by no means a small organization. Nor were they powerless. Since arriving on Earth, Norchek had encountered many members of the organization, and had received threats. ECF security took these seriously enough to assign a security detail, though Norchek insisted on using an Esool guard.

If Earth First was close to seizing control of the lightrail network, then things had escalated well beyond finding the lost colony. Everything was at stake now.

Norchek tapped the display in his desk and called Kellar, one of his lieutenants. "Admiral," Kellar answered.

"I am sending an encoded packet of data. I need you to carry it to the Esool home world on the very next outgoing vessel. We must waste no time."

"Yes Admiral," Kellar said.

The call ended and Norchek stood and walked out of his quarters. He made his way to the balcony of this floor, the large area that the ECF had customized for the Esool. Soil covered the entire deck, and plant life flourished everywhere. Large pools of water were provided so the Esool could enter and rejuvenate themselves as needed. Most importantly, the area was open to the sky. Norchek stood, eyes closed, bare feet digging into the soil, arms outstretched. The sun felt good on his skin, nourishing.

A calm came over him, and his thoughts became focused. All worry was put aside as a plan began to form.

CHAPTER 7

IT WAS TOUGH KEEPING UP WITH EDWARD. NOT ONLY DID HE levitate a couple of feet about the ground, and move at at a speed slightly above comfortable walking speed, he had a tendency to go *through* an object, rather than around it.

"Can you maybe just pretend like you have the same physical limits as the rest of us?" Penny asked, smiling and half-kidding.

"Sorry," Edward said. After that he moved around things instead of through them, but his pace was still a little on the brisk side.

He seemed to be curious about absolutely everything. No detail was too small, nothing was too mundane. For a while he floated serenely above a knotted and twisted tangle of wire, its insulation burned and melted into molten-looking warts of plastic. Worthless junk to most people. Fascinating to Edward.

Penny remembered being hung up on small details, while sharing headspace with Edward. Everything — absolutely *everything* — seemed important. Every detail *mattered*.

At the time, as her mind moved in long pulls of putty,

slow and indistinct in shape or purpose, it had been exhausting to notice it all. But she could see that nothing would tire Edward. He was pure energy, after all.

She, on the other hand, was starting to wear out.

"Do you think we could just sit for a while? Over there?" She nodded to one of the trees near the cluster of buildings used as research labs. Edward said nothing, but floated to them and came to rest on the ground. Penny soon joined him.

The breeze was light and cool in the shade, and Penny could feel the sweat start to dry on her neck and face. The brisk pace, through a winding path that meandered in and out of every part of the colony, had taken more out of her than she'd expected. She was used to being physically active, sometimes pretty intensely and for long stretches of time. She was a competitor, scaling rock faces that topped the charts for difficulty. A brisk walk, even for an hour or two, shouldn't wind her like this.

Clearly the last few weeks had taken a toll. She'd been more or less inactive, sitting for long stretches at a time, usually staring at something compelling — like a dent or a bolt in a piece of metal. Riveting stuff.

She glanced at Edward. The breeze, strong enough to sway the branches overhead, had no effect on him at all.

"You're not normal," Penny said.

Edward didn't speak for a second, and showed no signs of having heard her at all. After a moment, however, he finally said, "No, I guess not."

Penny smiled, turning to look straight ahead again. "You've probably heard that a lot in your life."

"When I was human, yes."

His answer chilled her a bit, and she shivered, rubbing her arms. " Aren't you still human? I mean, yeah, you're made of energy, you float above the ground, you can do some pretty cool things. But you're still a *person*, right?"

"We are many," Edward said. "The Current. I think we're not human. People ... maybe. I'm starting to understand what it means, I think."

"What does it mean?" Penny asked.

"I'm alive. The Current is alive. We never knew, before. We didn't understand. Even me, before. But becoming part of the Current has helped us understand."

Penny shook her head. "Talking to you makes me kind of dizzy, Edward. I thought it was bad when you were in my head, but you're at a whole new level of strange now."

They sat in silence for a moment, and then, suddenly, out of nowhere, Edward let out a sharp, loud, "Ha!"

It startled Penny, and she flinched. "What the hell, Edward?"

"I wanted to try it," he said.

Again there was a pause, and suddenly Penny couldn't help herself. She burst into giggles, leaning back against the tree, staring up into the the shifting pattern of light in the leaves.

When she looked at Edward, he was still looking ahead, but there was something strange and unexpected happening.

"You're *smiling*," she said, smiling a little herself.

"I'm practicing," Edward said. "Sort of. I remember how to smile, and when you started laughing it happened all on its own."

Penny leaned forward again, then reached out to touch Edward's shoulder. She hesitated, then finally made contact.

He felt ... *odd*. Not like she had expected. There was no tingle, no shock. But there was no sense of texture to his clothing, no variation in contours in his shoulder. He was simply *there*.

"I used to hate being touched," Edward said. "And the Current never knew what it meant. But all of that has changed, thanks to you."

"Me?" Penny said, drawing her knees up to her chest, clasping her hands around them. "How's that?"

"Being part of your mind taught me why it's important — having contact. I couldn't understand it before. Couldn't understand what I was feeling, or why."

"But you understand it now?" Penny asked.

"I'm getting there."

She nodded. He *was* getting there. She could see that. Everything about him was changing rapidly. He was developing a personality. Taking on a life.

Something occurred to her.

"What about the others?" Penny asked. "The other waveforms that the Current absorbed?"

"We're here," Edward said.

Again, Penny shivered. His answer was too strange. He was saying that he was Edward, but also the many. That could explain the sudden evolution of personality. He seemed far more mature than he should be, far more knowledgable and insightful. Maybe that was because there were a few adults rattling around in his mind.

"Can you hear them? Talk to them?" Penny asked.

"Not the way you're thinking. They don't think. The Current doesn't think the way you would recognize it. It's more basic than that. We understand things, we can organize data, we can ask questions, but we don't always understand what we know or what we ask. I'm getting better at it."

"You need to work on the pronouns though," Penny said.

Edward smiled again.

"So was that a real smile or did you decide it was time to smile?"

"Both," Edward said, and for the first time he turned to look directly into her eyes. "I never liked making eye contact before, either," he said.

"Edward, I love you, but you creep me right the hell out some times."

"Sorry," he said.

And again Penny laughed, shaking her head. "It's ok," she said. "Or I think it is. Honestly, I have no idea how to deal with all of this. But I think we're doing the best we can. We'll be ok," she said.

She glanced up to see him nod. It was light, subtle, subconscious. Whatever was happening within Edward, it was making him *more* human, not less.

Time, she thought. *Give it time.*

Just then a voice broke into the moment. "Edward?"

Penny and Edward looked up to see ...

"Mom?" Penny said.

Her mother and another woman were standing near the treelike, staring at them. Everything came back to Penny in a slow but deliberate flood. Her mother, but not her mother. "Dr. Menton," Penny said, correcting herself. "And ..."

"Mother," Edward said, as if this were the most normal thing in the world.

Dr. Ballar — the woman with Dr. Ballar's personality — rushed forward and knelt on the ground before him, but made no move to reach out. Penny realized that she was falling back on old patterns, coming close to her son but respecting his boundaries, keeping herself from reaching out to touch him, to hug him.

The autism had shaped her relationship to her son his entire life. Now, with the strangest of barriers between them, they were actually more free than they'd ever been. "Hug him," Penny said quietly.

Dr. Ballar looked at her, and there was a sort of pleading in her eyes, which were red and rimmed with tears.

"Hug him," Penny urged again.

And with that the last barrier fell, and a mother was reunited with her son in a moment they never could have had, over a hundred years ago.

MITCH WAS ABOUT **to lose it on Alan.**

Problem was, Alan wasn't actually doing anything wrong.

In fact, he was putting them ahead of schedule, making intuitive leaps in modifying the shuttle and the lightrail hub, making calculations in his head that Mitch would have struggled to make using a handheld. Mitch double checked, of course. But the most irritating thing about Alan was you didn't have to double check his work. He was always right. It was the most irritating thing about him.

There was a time, not long ago, that a little fact like that would make Mitch proud, not fill him with anger. Why couldn't he simply go back to that? Somar had pardoned Alan. Thomas, working beside him at one of the shuttles control terminals, was kidding him like always. The Blue Collars had fallen right back in their old routines with him. Everyone seemed to be able to forgive the kid.

Everyone but Mitch.

Alan had stranded them here. He'd gotten a lot of people killed, and hurt a lot more. He'd ruined a lot of lives. Maybe he hadn't intended it to go this way, but he'd definitely had a plan, and that plan lead straight to here.

"Can you bring up the relays from the pilot station?" Thomas asked.

Mitch nodded and sat in what he'd come to think of as "Reilly's seat." The mechanism was wild. The usual computer system was there, an interface he could touch and interact with. Normal. But all of these cables — all the physical movement it took to navigate this thing. Reilly was more like a dancer than a pilot. And no one could dance the way she could.

He missed her. How could he *miss* her? He'd just seen her maybe twenty minutes ago, and she was no more than a few hundred feet away at any given time. But there it was. He missed her. This was supposed to be their "honeymoon," and instead of spending it with her he was sitting in her seat, working side-by-side with the guy who got her hurt in the first place.

"All tangled up?" Thomas asked.

Mitch looked up, startled. "What?"

"The controls," Thomas nodded. "I'm still not used to how all of that works. I don't know if I could pilot this thing without popping a shoulder out of socket." He smiled, and Mitch caught himself smiling back.

It was nice, getting back to their "routine." So much had happened since the wedding, and both of them had faced some tough choices and tough situations lately. So it was a relief to share a joke with a friend.

If Mitch could claim anyone in the universe as his best friend, he supposed it would have to be Thomas.

He glanced at Alan, who was working at a station on the other side of the shuttle. Far from Mitch. As far as the space would allow. When Mitch looked his way, Alan quickly looked back to his work. He'd been watching the two of them. He'd seen the exchange, the smiles, the bond between Mitch and Thomas.

He wants me to forgive him, Mitch said.

He looked up to see Thomas tracking his gaze, eyebrows raising in an unspoken question.

"I can't," Mitch said.

Thomas, a light smile still on his lips that hinted at understanding too well, said nothing.

They continued making adjustments. Mitch brought the relay online, and the three of them walked through a startup sequence.

"It's a little janky," Thomas said.

Mitch and Alan stared at him.

"*Janky*. You know janky. Right?"

Silence.

Thomas looked at Alan, a pleading expression on his face. "C'mon! You're from my time. You've heard this."

Alan shrugged, and suddenly, without warning, Mitch burst out laughing. Immediately after, everyone else did too.

"What's so funny?" Reilly said as she stuck her head in through the side door.

"It's *janky*," Mitch said, and they all laughed again.

Reilly laughed too, but immediately clutched her ribs. Mitch felt all the joy and laughter fade from him then. Reality came back, and he was standing in a small space with the woman he loved, his best friend, and the kid who had betrayed them all.

The mood faded, and the room got quiet until someone else entered behind Reilly.

Taggart, his face flush with excitement, scanned the room until he saw Alan. "The simulation is finished," he said.

"What did it show?" Alan asked, with more emotion in

his voice than Mitch was used to hearing.

"Come see!"

Alan exchanged glances with Mitch, who nodded, and then he was off with Taggart.

"We're pretty much set here," Thomas said. "I need to check on a few things. Somewhere else."

"You're leaving the honeymooners alone?" Reilly asked.

"As delicately as one of them will let me," Thomas replied, smiling as he left, closing the door behind him.

"Well that was subtle," Mitch said.

"I don't have time in my life for subtle," Reilly said, springing forward and throwing her arms around his neck to pull him down into a kiss.

He knew it had to hurt. She winced slightly, but didn't make a sound. And rather than calling her out on it, Mitch enjoyed the kiss instead.

When they came up for air, they clung to each other in the embrace. Mitch was careful not to touch her sore ribs.

"How's it going?"

"Good," Mitch said, smiling.

"I meant with Alan. How are you?"

Mitch hesitated. "That's a little different," he said.

Reilly dipped her chin a bit while looking up at him, and Mitch felt his heart bounce from his ribcage. She could do that to him — get him with just a look.

"He's doing all the right things," Mitch said, a light note of disgust in his voice.

"But you kind of don't want him to?" she asked.

He grunted.

Reilly pulled away from him and leaned against the railing that surrounded the pilot's seat. She absently reached up and wound a hand through the control cables. Mitch worried for a moment that they would tangle, then realized they were safer in her hands than they would be under any other condition. She was as much a part of the shuttle as the engines, the navigation system, the comms.

"We have to get over it," Reilly said.

Mitch was surprised. "Get over it? Reilly, he …"

"Did what he did," she said. "Yeah, I was there."

"I just mean …"

"I know what you mean," she said, putting a hand on his chest. He was sure she could feel the thudding there. How could she miss it? "I'm mad at him too. But he was pardoned. And he's working really hard to fix what he did. Maybe he'll never be able to make up for it, but what good is it going to do us to hold on to all of this? Everyone else is letting it go."

"I'm not sure that's entirely true …"

"It's true," she said, digging her nails into his chest slightly.

He grunted, then smiled and laughed lightly. "So I guess my days of finishing a sentence are done," he said.

She smiled back, "Your last sentence was 'I do,'" she said. "The rest belong to me."

———

THOMAS HAD AN ULTERIOR MOTIVE. It was true he wanted to give the honeymooners their space. He could see it in Mitch — the constant yearning to get back to Reilly. She probably felt the same. She was giving him the space he needed to do the work, but she eventually broke down and showed up.

Beyond being an outstanding wingman, though, Thomas wanted to know what had Taggart and Alan all worked up.

Things were dicey with the two of them. Trust was an

issue, all around. Alan was trying hard, and Thomas could see he earnestly wanted to absolve himself of what he'd done. Taggart, on the other hand, was more of a question mark.

He was clearly different. Thomas hadn't had much time to interact with him when Louis was "in charge," which made him a little sad. He'd been busy at the time, with orbital platforms exploding and shuttles exploding and colony towers exploding — Thomas eyed his surroundings warily, wondering if he might have some sort of secret power of incendiary combustion.

He arrived at Alan's lab to find Alan and Taggart excitedly discussing something on a handheld. "Something cool?" he asked.

They turned to look at him, and each was wearing a boyish grin that turned out to be infectious. Thomas, also smiling, moved closer.

"We ran a simulation on data from my scans of the Current, using Mr. Taggart's entanglement protocols to see if we could create a sympathetic relationship."

"Just Taggart," Taggart said absently.

"Taggart," Alan corrected.

"And it worked?" Thomas asked.

Alan smiled. "It worked."

Thomas was stunned. He leaned in to inspect the data, and saw a basic visual representation of a human brain. A small segment was glowing. Alan tapped the screen and the simulation exploded outward (no combustions, thankfully), showing a sort of cartoon representation of the Current.

"The Current absorbs the waveforms by doing exactly what we're talking about here. It's easier to create sympathetic particles in the static data of the pods, though. With humans, it's trickier."

Alan brought up another image, this time the familiar cancellation wave. "When I implanted the First Colony waveforms, I exploited a vulnerability in the cancellation wave. When my parents worked out how to suppress the mind of a person in stasis, to keep them from becoming lucid during long flights, they took the cautious route. The whole cancellation wave works just like noise-canceling technology."

"Which works how, exactly?" Thomas asked cautiously.

Alan gave him a severe look, with a crooked half-smile. "'You never studied,'" he intoned.

"*Ghostbusters*? You're quoting *Ghostbusters*? Did someone cancellation wave the real Alan?"

"What's a ghostbuster?" Taggart asked.

"I'll tell you later," Alan said. "Noise-canceling technology generally works by creating a waveform that is exactly the same as an incoming waveform, with one exception — it's exactly 180 degrees out of phase with the original. The top and bottom of the wave match up when that happens, in an inversion. The two waveforms 'crash' into each other, and cancel out."

"I remember Louis explaining this to me, and I still don't quite get it."

"That's because you're more about the quantum physics and mechanics. But think of it like a lock and key. There are teeth on a key that match the tumblers on a lock. If you use the wrong key, the lock stays locked, because the teeth and the tumblers don't line up. If you use the right key, the teeth and tumblers match, and the key can turn. The cancellation wave is a key that locks the mind."

Thomas nodded. "The least simple explanation I've heard, but I think I get it."

"Good, because here's where things get really interesting," Alan said. "When mom and dad built the cancellation wave technology, they didn't want to risk shutting down someone's mind permanently. So they built a safeguard. There's a tiny part of the wave that stays active. It's so small that it can't start the thought process. It's just a tiny bit of memory or something. No one notices it. Or no one has in more than a hundred years of using stasis. You and I are pretty much living proof that you can be in stasis long-term and not become lucid."

"So there's a tumbler that the key doesn't trigger," Thomas said.

"Right," Alan said, smiling. "It was a hole in the system that I was able to exploit. I inserted the First Colony wave-forms into that spot, and when I activated the trigger the new waveform spread, basically disengaging all the tumblers, turning on the lock while taking over the whole mechanism."

"So what does this mean? How does this help?"

Alan and Taggart exchanged looks, grinning. Taggart was the one who spoke, "We can use the same exploit to our advantage. That unengaged tumbler, to use the metaphor. It's enough of a start that a being like the Current, who can see the waveforms directly, can latch on. It can identify anything that isn't directly connected to that tumbler, and absorb it."

Thomas, eyes widening, said, "So you did it! You found a way to restore everyone!"

"I think so, yeah. I can at least teach the Current how to tell the difference between the two waveforms. The suppression wave can be shut off easy enough. Separating the two active waveforms would be impossible for our technology, but the Current could do it."

Thomas felt like dancing, or laughing, or something

very unprofessional. He opted for hugging, reaching out to pull Alan in for a good, solid bro hug, just like the old days. Alan put up a bit of a struggle, but gave in eventually.

Taggart grinned, wide and large.

He really has changed, Thomas thought. *Maybe Louis is still in there.*

Alan finally managed to pull away, and scooped up the handheld. "I have to go find Edward. I have the scans in here. I can show it to him. He can mimic the waveform, I've seen him do that. And when he does, he can create a sympathetic particle. All it takes at that point is to absorb the waveform, and everyone goes back to normal!"

Alan was smiling and laughing and making his way to the door. Thomas smiled after him, nodded when Alan looked back, and was glad enough to send him on his way.

He didn't have the heart to point out the problem.

"You're thinking it," Taggart said, and Thomas turned to look at him.

"What?" Thomas said.

"You're thinking that the Current can remove the waveforms from the colonists, but then what?"

Thomas nodded. "Yeah, that's pretty much it. No matter what else happens, it seems like someone is going to be lost."

Taggart nodded, then shrugged. "Maybe. But give him a shot. He's brilliant, and he feels guilty as hell about all of this. It will occur to him, any minute now, that he's about to hand over the lives a few thousand souls. He won't take it lightly."

"He'll do it, though," Thomas said.

"He will," Taggart agreed.

Thomas regarded him. "What about you? Are you worried?"

"I was," Taggart said. "But then something occurred to me. I'm unique. I'm not being controlled by one of the First Colonists. I'm me, with a bit extra. Penny is completely free of Edward's waveform, as is Meyers. But my passenger is still here for the ride. And I think I like it that way."

Thomas looked at him for a long time. "What about Louis? Do you think he likes it that way?"

Taggart took a deep breath and let it out slowly. "I think he does, yes. I think he's at peace about all of this. That's how it feels, anyway. He's ... well, frankly, I think he's happy. He gets to see his son. He gets to work side by side with him. He's here," Taggart said, tapping his forehead. "Not separate, but not suppressed. We're together now. I think it might actually be too late to remove him, honestly."

"Too integrated?" Thomas asked.

Taggart nodded.

"But the others aren't in the same boat. So what's fair? The Current can apparently integrate the waveforms, make them go deeper. Maybe that would be better than absorbing them."

Taggart shrugged. "Maybe. With me it was accidental, though. With them it would be a choice. And since we can't ask the colonists, since only the First Colony souls are able to respond, we can't rely on what they say. The just thing to do is to remove them."

Thomas wasn't comfortable with this, but couldn't think of any fault in Taggart's reasoning.

"Let's hope we're right," Thomas said. He turned and left the room, and Taggart. He couldn't walk away from how he felt, though — that he was finally going to live up to what history thought of him.

Maybe history knew best.

CHAPTER 8

"How is the work coming, Mr. Garrison?" Somar asked as he approached the shuttle.

He was still feeling a bit unsteady, and was actively seeking a distraction from his physical discomfort. The healing process had been effective, but it was not without its side effects. Being healed by a bath of his own blood — it was unusual. Somar could not think of another instance of it in Esool history. Not in this manner.

"Everything's coming together, Captain," Mitch said. "We were able to retrofit the shuttle with the lightrail relay. Alan did some fantastic work there." This last bit had an edge to it that even Somar picked up on, though he chose to let it pass.

Somar inspected the work. The relay was mounted to the top of the shuttle, stitched in place with molecular disruption welding. The disparate metal pieces formed one solid component, and it was so well done as to seem part of the original design. "Could it survive entry onto the lightrail?" Somar asked.

Mitch shrugged. "The hope is it won't have to, if Taggart's communications protocols work."

Somar nodded. "You have reservations about both of the primary aspects of this plan, I see."

Mitch shook his head. "It doesn't matter, Captain. It's the plan we have. I'm onboard. I have no choice but to trust both of them. And as someone told me recently, everyone else has forgiven them. It does me no good to hold on to it."

Somar nodded, though he suspected that "holding on to it" was exactly what Mr. Garrison was doing. He was a consummate officer, however, dedicated and competent. He would not allow his personal feelings to jeopardize the mission.

Thomas arrived moments later. "Looking good," he said, admiring the welds. "You'd hardly believe this thing might shake us like a cup of dice until we're dead."

"*I'd* believe it," Mitch said.

To Somar's surprise and confusion, both men grinned broadly and laughed. He would never understand humans and their ability to turn even morose statements into humor. Though, he supposed, it was much like the Esool and their view of death. Rather than fear it, one should embrace it, and let it teach what it will.

Somar observed for a moment more as the two men discussed the shuttle and Taggart's communication protocols. "I will leave you to the details. I trust you will inform me if there are any changes."

Mitch nodded. "I think we're getting there. I want to run a full diagnostic on everything, go back over all of it, tighten every bolt, that sort of thing."

"I'll lend a hand," Thomas said, staring at the lightrail relay as he spoke. Somar suspected his interests were equally divided between assessing the condition of the vessel and exploring the technology up close.

"Very well," Somar nodded, and turned to leave.

Thomas caught up to him in a few steps.

"Captain, is everything ok? You seem more ... *reserved* than usual."

Somar looked at him, a small smile on his lips. "I am thinking of Captain Alonzo."

Thomas nodded, his expression suddenly pained. "I think about him quite a bit. Is he ... he's still in stasis?"

"Indeed," Somar said. "I have ordered Dr. Michaels to make arrangements for the pod to be stored long term."

"Long term?"

"We do not currently have the means to treat him, but I am hopeful that a treatment may still be developed. Perhaps in the future."

Again Thomas nodded. "I see. Well, that's possible. Isn't everything?"

"Indeed. However, his current condition weighs heavily on me. I feel responsible."

"You're not," Thomas said quickly. "If anyone is responsible, it's me."

"Mr. Paris, you are unmatched in your ability to assume responsibility for everything. In this instance, I believe you acted in the best interest of the colony. Your motives were altruistic and guided by an instinct of leadership. However, I cannot help but feel that I am alive at the expense of his life. A debt that can only be paid in blood."

Thomas was wary. "What do you have in mind?" he said.

Somar smiled. "Be calm, Mr. Paris. My intention is to perform the blood ceremony — a ritual of my people, to honor the fallen."

Thomas was clearly relieved. "Ok. Can I help? Is there anything I can do?"

"Not this time," Somar said. "Thank you."

Thomas nodded, keeping Somar's gaze as he turned to go back to the shuttle.

He is a dedicated man, Somar thought. *And more of a leader than he credits himself to be.*

Somar left then, and wound his way through the colony to the forest at its edge. He cut through to a clearing at the crest of a small hill, where the forest thinned and he could see the open sky above and the river in the valley below. He had discovered this spot some time ago, and had returned to it often. It reminded him of his home on the Esool home world, where had been born. He had matured in a spot very much like this one.

From a small pouch on his side, he removed one of the multi-tools issued by the ECF. He rotated the dial to draw out a small, sharp knife blade. This was far from the ceremonial blade he would have preferred, but such things were currently beyond his reach. Perhaps after the Hidalgo mission, all of their lives would return to familiar patterns. He doubted this, however. The past few weeks had left a permanent mark on every soul in the colony, his included. Things had changed, and they would remain so.

Somar spread his hands wide and tilted his head upward. He felt the sun, its energy flowing into him, fueling him. He felt a light breeze in the air, and heard the sound of rustling leaves in the trees.

He bowed his head now, bring his hands together to clasp the knife, blade pointing down. With a swift motion he knelt and plunged the blade into the soil before him. He then bowed so that his palms touched the ground directly. He murmured ancient words, which were etched into his mind after decades of practice. Too many decades, too much practice. This was a prayer for the fallen, and he'd said it too often for his taste.

He now clasped the knife with his right hand and drew it from the soil. With another quick motion he drew the blade across his left forearm, a small cut but enough for blood to flow freely. He placed the flat of the blade on his forearm, coating it with green blood. He held the knife up to the sky again, letting the sun warm it, and then plunged it back into the soil. A return to the world. A gift of life in exchange for the life that had fallen.

Somar finished the ceremony, standing and brushing dirt from his knees. He cleaned the blade of the knife and rotated it back into a safe position, putting it back into its case. The cut on his arm was already healing and closing.

Everything returns, as if nothing ever happened, he thought. *Perhaps it will be the same for this colony.*

He turned to walk back to the others, but suddenly felt an intense pain in his stomach, like a sudden blow. It was enough to bring him to his knees, and nearly made him vomit from its intensity. He found himself out of breath, his head swimming and his vision going dark at the edges as he struggled for air.

When it finally subsided, Somar knelt on the ground much as he had for the blood ceremony. He took several deep breaths, feeling his body right itself from within.

He recognized this feeling.

Not here, he thought. *I am far from my people, far from my home. This is not the place.*

But he knew that these things did not wait for the right place or the right time. They happened as they happened — part of the cycle of life, even for the long-lived Esool. Somar had known that this day would come. It was overdue, in many ways.

The words of Nolad came to mind.

"The wise know that the end of a path is also its beginning."

EDWARD HAD FINALLY CONVINCED **his mother** that she should return to her work and let him and Penny continue their exploration of the colony. "It helps me," he said. A simple phrase, but one his mother recognized as Edward asking her to give him space, to let him figure something out on his own. It was a sort of code or shorthand they had used, back when he was a human boy.

It might have been a little manipulative to use it now, but Edward really did need the space. He was exploring more than just the colony. He was feeling out exactly who he was now, and his role in the universe. His mother, even as a waveform inhabiting a different body, was too much of a reminder of his old self.

"She can tell you're different," Penny said.

"Yes," Edward said as they moved away. He was still hovering, but closer to the ground now. It could appear he was walking, if one didn't look closely. It helped make people more comfortable when he was around.

He was starting to pick up on things like that — the way people felt in his presence. He'd never had to worry about it before.

"So now what?" Penny asked. "More random exploring?" She didn't sound thrilled.

Edward stopped and turned to face her — another trick he'd learned, to keep people at ease. Ironically, eye contact was something his mother had constantly reminded him of before all of this. "I'm searching for something, but I'm not sure how to explain it."

Penny looked at him for a moment. "Just start. We'll figure it out as we go."

Edward wasn't sure he could "just start." There was so much. What was the most basic thing? "We are one who is many, but we want to just be the many."

Penny studied him, then said, "The other personalities, the ones you absorbed. You want to separate them. We know that."

"So I am looking."

"You think you'll find a way to separate everyone some- where here in the colony?"

Edward struggled with this. "Yes. Or no."

"Maybe?" Penny suggested.

"Maybe. There may be a way here. We think the lightrail might be the way."

Penny's eyes widened. "What do you mean? How could the lightrail help?"

This was the part that Edward couldn't quite explain. There were bits and pieces in his mind — information he had gleaned from the personalities he'd absorbed, from Penny, from Taggart. There were the scans Alan had shared with him. But all of this formed a pile, not a mountain. Edward was struggling to fit pieces together in a way that made sense. He couldn't quite describe why he felt that the lightrail was the key. Most might call it "instinct."

He was about to articulate this to Penny when Alan came rushing toward them, waving a handheld in the air.

"Edward!" he cried. He stopped in front of them, huffing a bit "I've been cooped up ... in a cell ... too long," he said, smiling.

Penny was also smiling, though Edward thought she

might not be aware. Edward's ability to see different spectrums, to see the ebb and flow of energy in humans, was still new enough that he didn't fully understand what he was seeing. He could pick up stray thoughts — signal leakage, perhaps — if he was physically close to someone. With Penny, he was much more finely attuned to her thoughts than anyone else. And so he discovered that Penny's feelings for Alan were stronger than she realized. He could see it in her aura. She literally lit up when he was around.

"Did you find something? About Edward?" Penny asked, and Edward could hear and see worry in her. He felt touched by her concern. They were close. He'd never been close to anyone before.

"I found everything," Alan said, beaming.

He explained the simulation and its results, showing them the handheld. Edward saw more than just the display. He could see the patterns of energy pulsing through the device. He could see the patterns made by the data. And what he saw made him feel very excited. Because there was more there than Alan suspected.

Edward could absorb the First Colony waveforms, and restore the colonists to normal. Beyond that, however, Edward saw something else — something he had not expected. The data was a roadmap. The answer was right here.

"But what about the First Colonists?" Penny asked.

It was as if a stormcloud fell over Alan's features. His smile instantly faded, and his eyes became unfocused and sad.

"How could I not think of that?" he asked quietly. He lowered his hands to his side, and his shoulders slumped. "How many times?" he asked, staring at the ground. "How many times will I doom these people?"

Penny stepped forward and put her hands on Alan's shoulders. "You're trying to help," she said, firmly. "And it's the right thing to do."

"How can you say that?" Alan said. "They'll be gone! If we do this, they're gone for good!"

Penny hugged him, and the two stood in the embrace for a time, silent.

"They won't be gone," Edward said.

They looked at him, questioning. "They'll be part of the Current. And I believe I know how to separate them. I believe I know how to give them all life."

Penny and Alan exchanged looks, and Penny cautiously asked, "How, Edward? What are you thinking?"

Edward knew what he would have to do, though it was a risk. "I can save them all," he said. And with that he seemingly disappeared.

Far from being gone, however, he was in the energy form of the Current. He'd become an invisible field that could move unseen and unnoticed, as the Current had during those weeks prior to revealing itself to the humans.

This time, however, the Current was not moving in a concentrated mass of energy. Instead, it was spread thin, covering the entirety of the colony, touching everything at once — every mind at once.

And there they were.

Every soul in the colony was visible to the Current, and thanks to Alan's simulation it now knew how to recognize that small bit of the original colonist. It could trace the pattern of each mind, and with a nudge, the smallest of effort, it could split the original from the waveform that was integrated with it.

In an instant, every First Colonist personality was free from its host. For a brilliant second, all were independent, all knew freedom. Even those that had already been absorbed into the Current tasted that freedom.

It came with distance. The thinner the Current could spread, the easier it was for the individual waveforms to take shape, to pull free.

The problem was power.

The Current's natural energy wasn't enough. It couldn't spread out far enough to weaken the bond and give the waveform the chance to pull free without dissipating altogether. The very act of freeing the minds trapped within the Current would bring death to them all. An entire species would be wiped out before it had even begun to live.

But it was close — so very close.

In anguish, the Current pulled back together, once again taking the form of Edward, whose personality reasserted itself. He was floating now, several feet above the ground, unnaturally static and unmoving.

"Edward!" Penny cried.

"Are you ok?" Alan asked.

They dared not touch him, but instead stood a couple of feet away, looking worried.

Edward came back to himself, and straightened. He lowered himself closer to the ground, and looked directly at Penny. "It didn't work," Edward said. "It almost did, but it wasn't enough."

"What did you do?" Penny asked, stepping closer. She put a tentative hand out toward him, and Edward remembered to dampen his ambient energy field before she made contact.

"It almost worked," Edward said again. "But I know now what I have to do."

"What?" Alan asked. "What do you have to do?"

Edward looked at him and said, "I have to be everywhere."

"ABSOLUTELY NOT," **Mitch told Reilly.**

"You go, I go," Reilly said. "You nearly died ... like six times or something ..."

"Twice," Thomas said. "Three times if you count the crash."

"Not helping," Mitch said, giving him a severe look.

"*Three times*," Reilly said, her voice rising. "And now we're married. If you think I'm going to let you go rushing off to maybe blow yourself up without me, you weren't paying attention to the vows."

"Actually," Thomas said, "I don't think the whole 'til death do you part' thing means you have to die *together*."

"*Not. Helping.*" Mitch said, his teeth clenched.

Reilly punched Mitch in the arm. "I'm *going*," she said, and with that she stepped into the shuttle.

"Great," Mitch said. "It's going to take an hour to pry her out of there now."

"Or," Thomas said, "you could just give up and let her go."

Mitch blinked. "Are you insane?"

"Maybe," Thomas said, smiling. "But no more than the guy who's trying to tell his wife, who happens to be the best pilot we have, that he's going to go risk his life while she sits here on the ground waiting to hear that he's dead."

"I ..." Mitch started, but suddenly clamped his jaw shut. After a moment he said, "Dammit."

Thomas laughed and chucked him on the shoulder. "Don't worry about it," he said. "Between the three of us, I think we have things covered. I think it's time you cut your losses and accept the inevitable."

"Good advice," Somar said from behind them. "And in that vein, Mr. Paris, I trust you will accept that you will not be participating in the mission."

Thomas and Mitch turned to see the Captain, both of their jaws hanging. "Wait, what?" Thomas asked. "I'm *grounded*?"

"Indeed," Somar said.

"Sir," Mitch said, "we prepped this mission with the intention of having me onboard for mechanical and Thomas onboard for the comms. If he doesn't go, we're a man short. I don't know enough about the protocols to make this work."

"Understood, Mr. Garrison. That is why you will be taking Mr. Angelou with you."

Silence. Mitch could hardly believe what he'd just heard. In fact, he absolutely *could not* believe it. "Sir?" he asked, his throat dry.

"Mr. Angelou will accompany you on this mission. He is more than qualified. And I have need of Mr. Paris here on the surface."

"Captain," Thomas said, "I don't understand. Has something happened?"

"These are my orders," Somar said, and then turned to leave.

Thomas exchanged a look with Mitch as Somar walked away. "What just happened?" he asked.

Mitch wasn't sure. The only thing he knew for certain was that his injured wife and the guy who caused everything they were dealing with would be locked in a shuttle with him, floating at the edge of space as they activated technology cobbled together from spare parts. What could possibly go wrong with *that* scenario?

"I'm going to see if I can get any more info," Thomas said, following Somar.

"I'll be here," Mitch said, "waiting for the moon to fall on my head or something."

"Go kiss the girl," Thomas said, not even looking back.

Mitch decided that was as good an idea as any. He turned to step into the shuttle, and noticed the interior lights brighten and then dim.

Power fluctuations already, he thought. It seemed like a bad sign.

CHAPTER 9

Somar entered his quarters, just off of the space he used as an office and strategy room. The room was well lit by skylights above, custom built to allow as much sunlight into the room as possible, regardless of the time of day. He preferred it this way. Artificial light eventually made him feel weary, cooped up. The sun was a welcome companion to an Esool.

He walked to the small table at one end of the room. Previously it had served as a desk, but at present it supported a small potted sapling. It was an Earth species, known as a "white oak." According to the data record associated with its stasis cylinder, this species grew to immense size, and was quite strong, with roots that spread wide. Those roots could penetrate even solid stone, given time.

This seemed fitting, for the purpose Somar had in mind. A symbol of strength and persistence, beautiful and long-lived. His scans of the sapling revealed it would serve well. Its maturation cycle had been accelerated by genetic modification, so it could grow quickly on a colony world. The modified cycle was not a perfect match, but it was close enough for Somar's purposes.

He checked to ensure the graft had taken, that it was responsive to his blood. The antibodies in his bloodstream could heal plant matter much faster than human flesh, and in a very short time the graft became indistinguishable from rest of the sapling. Somar hefted it from the table by the small planter, admiring it, checking to ensure everything was as it should be. He then encapsulated it once again in the cylinder and activated stasis.

There was a knock on the door from outside. Somar placed the stasis cylinder back on the table and answered the door to find Thomas standing there. He ushered him inside.

"It may actually be brighter in here than it is outside," Thomas said, blinking.

Somar smiled. "How may I help you, Mr. Paris?"

Thomas looked at him for a moment, then asked, "Why do you do that?"

Somar blinked. "I'm not certain what you mean."

"Why call me 'Mr. Paris?' You only do it when we're in private, or when we're around someone who knows my secret. But you also refer to everyone that way. 'Mr. Garrison.' 'Mr. Taggart.' For some reason you still refer to Alan as 'Mr. Angelou," even though you known *his* real name."

"I must point out that you and the others, including Mr. Angelou himself, continue to refer to him by his chosen name."

"And everyone calls me Thomas."

"Indeed. Which is, in fact, your name."

Thomas smiled, and laughed lightly. "Fair enough. But why the formality all the time? Why not just use our first names, like we do? I do occasionally call you Somar."

"I have noted this. And as you are not formally in the chain of command I have determined there is no violation of protocol."

Somar looked at him intently, and Thomas seemed a little stunned for a moment. Finally Somar allowed himself to smile.

Again Thomas laughed.

"Mr. Paris ... *Thomas* ... I use your given surname as a sign of my respect for you. Surnames are not something my people use. Instead, we may talk of lineages. Houses. When appropriate, we show our respect for an individual by addressing him with the name of his house. I'm aware, however, that human customs differ on this."

"Not entirely," Thomas said. "We have similar customs on Earth. Or we did in my time. Honorifics, like 'President' or 'Professor' or 'Doctor.' Sometimes those honorifics would be used even by close friends, as a sign of respect. So I think I understand."

Somar nodded. "Was there anything I could help you with, Thomas?"

A light smile played on his lips, and Thomas replied, "Not particularly. I was concerned about your change to our plan. You were a little more abrupt than usual, and I thought maybe something was wrong."

Somar waved to a chair, offering Thomas a seat as he took one of his own. Thomas sat, immediately crossing his legs, bringing up one ankle to rest on the opposing knee. Another human custom Somar did not understand. The pressure on the lower back must be immense.

"I apologize if my orders have created discord, but I felt it was necessary for you to remain here, with the colony."

"Care to say why?" Thomas asked.

Somar started to answer, then stopped. Instead he stood

and stepped to the table, picking up the stasis cylinder. He carried it to Thomas, handing it to him with a bit of formality.

"What's this?" Thomas asked, taking the cylinder.

"It is a 'white oak.' Earth species flora. We have several such saplings in stasis, stored in the Citadel module."

Thomas arched his eyebrows. "Have you been researching Earth customs? I can see the confusion, but most people give flowers."

"I'm aware," Somar said, smiling. "However, this is not a token of affection. Or rather, it is not *strictly* a token of affection. I would like for you to care for this, and to plant it on my behalf."

"On you're behalf? Is this a ceremony of some sort?"

"In its way. I have encoded details in the memory of the module. At a specific time of year, which I have noted, I wish for you to take it to the designated coordinates and plant it. I have also left instructions for its care and future needs."

Thomas looked alarmed. "Somar, what the hell is going on here?"

Somar once again took his seat. "Thomas, of all humans here, I feel closest to you. Perhaps it is your age."

"Hey!"

"It could also be our bond of blood. However, I believe it is because you are a uniquely strong individual. Your character is without equal. You are, in every way, one of the most fit leaders I have ever met."

Thomas had turned his head away in embarrassment, his expression unreadable to Somar.

"I'm touched. And honored," Thomas said, a small catch in his voice. "This means a great deal, coming from you. But I really don't know where this is going."

Somar took a breath, and said, "I would like for you to lead this colony."

Again Thomas looked surprised. "I think the job is taken, and by someone far more qualified than me."

"None is more qualified. You are singularly the most responsible human I have ever met. Your character dictates that you put the needs of others above your own, at all costs. That is a trait I believe this colony will need."

"But you're our leader, Somar. Unless ... are you planning to leave? I can understand that. I guess I hadn't thought much about it, but once we've re-established contact with the ECF and the Esool, it would only makes sense. But it would make me and a lot of other people sad to see you go. You're a part of this colony. You're family."

"I feel very much the same, and I will be a part of this colony for the remainder of my life," Somar said.

Thomas looked relieved. "Good! And the Esool live for hundreds of years, right? So that's quite a commitment." He smiled at his joke, but after a moment the smile faded, replaced eventually by alarm. "Somar ..."

Somar slowly held up a hand, a sign that there was no need to say anything. There was a long silence in the room.

"How long?" Thomas finally asked, his voice a rasp in his throat.

"Dr. Michaels is unable to determine the time I have. My Esool physiology makes it difficult for him. But by my own experience, I believe it will be soon."

Thomas reached up to wipe away a tear that had collected, and which was instantly replaced by another. "I see," he said, then gave a small cough. "I see."

"I can think of none I would trust more than you, to take the role of leader in this community," Somar said.

Thomas nodded, saying nothing.

"There are other ... responsibilities. Things that I must entrust to you. I've left detailed instructions. I apologize for burdening you, but I have no one else."

"Of course," Thomas croaked. "No, of course. Anything."

"Good," Somar said. "If you please, I would prefer to keep this information quiet."

Thomas nodded. "Yes, of course. No problem."

Somar nodded, smiling, pleased. He stood, and Thomas stood with him.

"I believe the human custom is to 'shake on it,'" Somar said, extending his hand.

Thomas pushed the hand aside and gripped Somar by the shoulders. "I am going to hug you," he said, his voice broken and burdened with emotion. And then, true to his word, he did. And Somar did not mind.

"THAT WOULD PROBABLY BE AN INCREDIBLY **bad idea**," Alan said.

Edward was hovering toward the shuttle, where he hoped to talk to Mitch, Thomas, and Somar, and convince them to let him go along on the mission. Penny and Alan were trying to keep pace with him as he went. He could easily have just "decided" to be at the shuttle in an instant, to move as the Current could move, but after absorbing all of the waveforms in the colony he was feeling a bit unstable. They hadn't yet coalesced into the whole. They wanted to know where they were, and what was happening, and Edward had no way to comfort or calm them.

Penny helped him think. Having her close by helped him feel more confident about what he had to do. "Why?" he asked.

Alan raised the handheld as they walked. "Let me run a simulation. It would only take a day or so. We can figure out if this plan would work. I don't know what would happen to you, if you left the atmosphere. I *really* don't know what would happen if you came into contact with the lightrail."

Penny sprinted ahead and turned to face Edward. "You can't do this," she said.

Edward stopped and looked at her. "Why?" he asked.

"Because it might hurt you," she said, her voice small and afraid.

Edward looked at her. Really *looked* at her. He was getting better at reading the auras of humans. The spectrum of emotion told a lot about them, if you paid close enough attention. He could dip into her thoughts as well, get an impression of what was going on in her mind. But he didn't need that. He could tell. She was telling him directly, and he was becoming better able to understand. Better every moment.

"It might," he said.

"It probably would," Alan said, catching up to them. "The level of power in that network, Edward. It's unbelievable. It would be like trying to absorb a star. More than one, maybe."

"I'm not going to absorb it. I'm going to become a part of it."

"It won't matter," Penny said. "One will mean the other, right?"

Edward knew what she meant, but also knew that he had very little choice. He couldn't explain, to Penny or anyone, what was going on inside the Current. All those minds, all those souls, and all they wanted was to be individuals. He had freed the colonists, but at the expense of thousands of lives. Those lives were demanding their due.

A Blue Collar came running to them. "Alan!"

Alan turned toward her, surprised.

The Blue Collar hesitated when she saw Edward, but turned her attention back to Alan and said, "Captain Somar sent me with orders. He says you're on the Hidalgo mission."

Alan's eyes widened. "I am?"

"He ordered Thomas to stay behind," the Blue Collar said.

"I bet Thomas is thrilled about that," Penny said.

"Do you know why?" Alan asked.

The Blue Collar shook her head. "Just passing along orders. You're supposed to report directly to the shuttle. They're prepping to leave in an hour."

Alan turned to look at Penny and Edward. "I have to go," he said, but then turned to face Edward directly. "Please," he said. "Give this time. Once we're up, I can run scans, start the simulation. I can determine how this will affect you. And the lightrail, actually. Once we've established a connection, we can maintain it. You can go up later, once we know it's safe."

"Please listen to him," Penny said.

Edward looked from one to the other, and nodded. Penny looked relieved, and Alan returned the nod before running off with the Blue Collar, toward the shuttle.

Penny reached out and took Edward's hand. It was a somewhat automatic gesture. Edward could feel it, however. Not the pressure of it, or the texture of her hand — not the way most people would feel it. It was more like a gentle push against the electromagnetic field that Edward used to maintain his form. But he had thousands of memories of hands holding hands, and he knew what it *should* feel like. And, once recognized, that memory became the reality, and he actually *could* feel her hand in his.

"Thank you," Penny said. "What will you do now?"

"I need to think," he said. "Alone."

She withdrew her hand. "Ok. I can see how that might be the case. But please, don't pull away, ok? Don't just be isolated. We're all in this together. I want to help."

"Isolated," Edward said. "No, I don't feel isolated. And thank you, Penny. I know you want to help. I'll be back. Go see your mother and father."

She nodded, still looking a bit worried. She gave him a last, pleading look as she turned to walk away.

While she wasn't looking, Edward dispersed his EM field, functionally becoming invisible. The Current's natural state. Penny glanced back once, and hesitated when she realized he was gone, but soon turned and kept walking.

In "Current mode," Edward felt like he was no longer *Edward*. He could still think, and he could still direct what the Current did, but without his "physical" form to concentrate his thoughts he tended to "drift." He could move as the Current had moved, being nearly anywhere in an instant. He could see and feel and taste the energy of things around him, noticing it much more than he had while in his Edward form. He could see how difficult it would be for any other personality to exert itself. His unique perspective, as an autistic, had given him an advantage.

But he could see now, in this form, that it was a dwindling advantage. With all of the First Colony personalities absorbed into the Current's matrix, it would only be a matter of time before he became just one more struggling voice in the crowd. He could see, now, that he was already fading. Soon, the Current would revert to a sort of uniform state, and his personality would become inert — just one more among the many.

Unless he acted *now*.

He knew Alan was right. The smart play was to let them establish the lightrail connection and run scans and simulations, to determine how things would work and what could go wrong. He knew that this was the way humans preferred to approach something new. They wanted to be *certain* before acting on a plan. They wanted to eliminate all risk, as much as possible. Operating this way took time — and time was something the Current did not have.

With a thought, Edward directed the Current to the shuttle. He hovered nearby, invisible. As he watched, Mitch and Thomas were talking with Somar, who gave orders that made neither of them happy — especially Mitch. Once Somar left, Thomas followed, seeking answers. Mitch watched him go, then turned to enter the shuttle.

Edward acted.

In an instant he was onboard the shuttle, just before Mitch stepped through the door. The Current's ability to move from place to place had the side effect of spiking his ambient energy field for an instant, and as he came aboard there was a small surge in the shuttle's electrical grid. Mitch turned just at the wrong instant, and saw the lights brighten.

If Edward still needed to breathe, he would be holding his breath now. But Mitch seemed to shrug off the flareup, and continued inside with only a brief pause.

Edward, relieved, followed, and hid himself in a corner of the main crew compartment. Here he would stay, watching and listening.

He saw when Alan came aboard, and saw how tense things were between him and Mitch. They barely made eye contact, which Edward was more aware of than he'd been in the past. Watching the two of them as they went through pre-launch, he was struck by a feeling a *discomfort*.

Empathy, he thought. *I'm feeling empathy.*

The realization excited him, because he had never really understood what it meant to feel the way others felt. His experience, as part of the Current, had changed him. Ironically, in some ways it made him more *human*. All his life, Edward's autism had defined him, to others as much as to himself. Now, strangely, it had given him the means to create a *new* definition of himself. If he could experience empathy, then he could learn and grow. He could be more than Edward, the autistic boy. More than the Current, the one who was many.

Just *what* he would become was still uncertain. But he took solace in knowing that whatever or whoever it was, he would be able to *choose*.

All of these thoughts fluttered around in his mind, loosely connected threads that had to occasionally be gathered together to be understood. There were interjections from the subconscious minds of the other personalities within the Current, and they proved to be mostly insights and encouragement and comfort. And then, because the subconscious inevitably returns to the wants and needs of every soul, there came thousands of impulses, yearning for life and for freedom. The waveforms, barely conscious but still aware at their deepest level, wanted to be "selves" again. And they were asking — *When? When?*

As Edward watched and waited, as the prelaunch was completed and the shuttle rose into the air — bound for orbit, bound to connect with the lightrail — he whispered back to all of them. *Soon*, he said. *Soon*.

"Shuttle, this is command," Thomas said over comms.

"Go ahead, Thomas," Mitch replied.

"So we're not going to use code names?" Thomas asked. "I kind of didn't get to do this on the first mission I launched."

Mitch rolled his eyes. "Go ahead ... *command*." He could picture Thomas smiling, maybe doing a little fist pump. The idiot.

"We've got green lights across the board here in command central shuttle. You are good for launch, roger wilco charlie."

"What the hell are you talking about?" Mitch asked.

"No idea. I never learned any of the radio chatter stuff. You're good to go, Mitch," Thomas said.

Mitch nodded. Thomas was in rare form. Funny. Lightening the mood with banter. It helped keep the tension down in the shuttle, which was probably why he was doing it.

But Mitch couldn't help thinking something was *off*. There was a tone, some unspoken burden in the voice coming from comms. He'd have to talk to him when they were back.

If they came back.

"Roger that," Mitch said, mentally kicking himself for the lapse. "Reilly, let's get her up there."

"*Roger that*," Reilly mocked.

Alan laughed, and Mitch shot him a look. Things still weren't "cool" between them. But here he was, and here Mitch was. Reilly had taken it all in stride, Thomas hadn't put up much of a fight, and it was starting to feel a lot like Mitch was the only one holding on to the animosity.

Maybe I am, Mitch thought. *Maybe I'm holding a grudge just to hold a grudge.* He turned his attention to the readings, choosing to focus on the mission.

Reilly worked the controls like a master, and in seconds

the shuttle was in the air, smoothly arcing its way into the upper atmosphere. Within moments the sky darkened, the blue faded to black, and the stars popped into existence, one by one.

They broke atmosphere without a hitch.

"Man, that was tricky," Reilly said.

"What?" Mitch asked. "Looked like a perfect launch to me," he said.

"Oh, it was," she smiled. "But I had to work for it. The relay is throwing off this girl's whole balance."

"The shuttle's inertial dampeners and repulsor engines compensate for the weight and drag, so you shouldn't feel any difference," Alan said.

Reilly laughed, "I feel it, trust me."

They continued to move out and away from the planet, and finally into a stationary orbit. The shuttle settled in, Reilly made a few adjustments to the controls and said, "We're in geosync."

Alan and Mitch got busy.

Mitch checked all of the readings for the relay, using external cameras and sensors to determine if everything was still where it was supposed to be. Even a tiny shift in the relay's position could shred the shuttle in orbit once the lightrail connection was established. After a long pause he said, "Good to go."

Alan checked the interface, running quick diagnostics on the relay and on ships systems. "Good here," he said.

Mitch activated comms. "Command, this is shuttle, delta beta epsilon," he smirked at Reilly who rolled her eyes. "Ok, that joke's played out."

"How's it looking, Mitch?" Thomas responded. "You guys all set?"

"All set."

"Ok, shuttle. Give it a go, and try not to blow anything up, ok? You and your hobbies."

Mitch turned his head and looked at Alan, who nodded. He looked back at Reilly who was waiting patiently. "Do it," Mitch said.

Reilly made a few quick gestures and then hit a control from her console.

There was a sudden and very audible hum, starting small and low but gradually building, revving up like a cooling fan. Then, abruptly it leveled off and settled into a low register, barely audible.

Mitch hadn't realized how perfectly still he'd been, and as he slowly looked around he realized that both Reilly and Alan were holding their exact poses as well. "Did we live?" he asked.

"I'm no expert," Reilly said, "but I think at the very least we didn't die."

Mitch smiled.

"Shuttle systems stable," Alan said. "Relay is online and ..." he tapped the screen, then smiled. "Stable. We're in. We're connected to the lightrail."

Mitch blinked, unsure what he should say. As it turned out, he didn't have to say a thing.

Reilly suddenly leapt from the pilot's station, somehow untangling herself instantly from the flight controls. She grabbed Mitch around the neck, whooping and cheering. Mitch cheered back, and hugged her, trying not to bump the ribs, which Reilly seemed to not care about at the moment.

They hugged, they kissed, they whooped in celebration. And from the corner of his eye Mitch caught Alan standing close, smiling.

That was when it finally happened. Something within Mitch gave in, let go, turned a corner. On a whim he reached out and pulled Alan into a side hug as Reilly laughed and wrapped her arms around both of them.

"We're still not totally cool," Mitch said, though he was smiling.

Alan nodded, choked a bit. "No, it's ok. I get it."

They broke it up. "Back to stations," Mitch said. "We still have a job to do."

Alan rushed to comms. "On it," he said, and started initiating Taggart's protocol. In a few seconds the main screen changed and Mitch saw a strange and startled looking Blue Collar comms officer.

"Hello ..." Mitch started, then turned to Alan. "Who are we calling again?"

"Earth," Alan said, grinning. "Earth Colony Fleet."

Mitch smiled and shook his head. "Hello, ECF! This is Mitch Garrison of the colony vessel Citadel. We have never been happier to see a strange face."

"Citadel? As in the colony vessel that disappeared? Are you back? In orbit?"

"Not even close!" Mitch laughed, and Reilly and Alan joined him. "It's a very long story, and I will be more than happy to buy you a beer or twenty and tell you the whole thing. But first I need to put you in touch with our ground control. I'm also sending you some coordinates to where we are in the universe."

Mitch transmitted the coordinates and immediately saw a strange look on the Blue Collar's face. "This is a joke," he said.

"Yes it is," Mitch said. "The most unfunny joke I can think of. Now, why don't you discuss the punchline with my friend Captain Somar." With that Mitch transferred comms to ground control.

Again they whooped and cheered. It was a perfect

moment, and the three of them had risked everything to make it happen. But it had paid off. Here they were, in orbit around a world that they thought might be their grave some day. And, well, maybe it still might. Despite everything, Mitch had taken a bit of a shine to colony life. Maybe ...

There was a sudden jolt, and alarms erupted all over the shuttle's interior.

"Report!" Mitch yelled, getting himself settled and bringing up scans of the relay. Had it broken loose? Were they coming apart? Were they about to die?

"Energy surge!" Alan said.

"This is impossible," Reilly said. "These are the same readings you get when a ships makes the jump to lightrail!"

"What's happening?" Mitch shouted. "Did either of you initiate the jump?"

"No!" Reilly shouted.

Again there was a jolt, and Mitch looked from Reilly to Alan, who looked panicked. "It's him," Alan said.

"Who? Who is it?" Mitch asked.

Before Alan could answer the shuttle lurched one final time, and suddenly they were all engulfed in a searing burst of light and energy.

And then they were gone.

CHAPTER 10

Edward had waited patiently while everyone told jokes. He knew that impatience was something he'd have to master somehow. Not everything could move at the speed of light. But *he* could. And if they'd hurry up, he could get to it.

They did their scans and diagnostics and checks, they gave each other the nod, and then they started the relay.

Edward watched in the way only he could watch. He saw the cascade of energy from the relay — a pulse that sliced through the sky, reaching outward until, inevitably, it made contact with the network. He saw the flow of energy back down the line, strengthening their tentative beam, making it part of the larger network.

The lightrail was a beam of potent energy, creating localized wormholes, making it possible for a vessel to travel from star to star without burning through multiple lifetimes. It was threaded through a network of hubs and relays that strengthened it, extending its reach, allowing it to expand exponentially. It was a technological marvel, and an architecture beyond anything humanity had ever achieved before.

It was *beautiful*.

The others were celebrating, but their cheers were nothing compared to the joy Edward felt. He studied the pattern of energy in the lightrail, and understood it for what it was — *freedom. Independence. Life*. Everything the Current hoped for would be found there, in those winding tendrils of energy that were only visible to humans as they traveled. Edward could see them all the time.

He moved, invisibly, through the shuttle. The hull was internally grounded, and would give him some trouble if he tried to phase through. But there were other paths he could take. He made his way to a small window in the crew chamber door. The glass was thick, and worked as an insulator, but the seal around it was just conductive enough to allow him through.

The moment of truth. Would he be able to survive in space? Could he survive away from the planet, the Current's home world?

There was only one way to find out.

He pressed against the glass, and like water he leaked through the seal and out into space. In a moment, he was completely outside of the shuttle.

He had survived.

And there it was.

With no atmosphere to distort his vision, he could see it clearly. Raw energy, stretching beyond his field of vision and into a deep inkwell of night. It was so tightly woven that it looked "smooth" to him. No ambient energy leaked from it. Not even a stray electron. It was *perfect*.

He moved closer, and as he did he could feel himself drawn to it, like a magnet. He moved faster. There was no turning back now. There was no desire to. There was only the lightrail.

He made contact, and everything changed.

Suddenly he was no longer outside the shuttle, but was instead at a lightrail hub lightyears away.

From his experience and the knowledge gained by interacting with the humans, he knew that it sometimes took many weeks to move to a lightrail hub along the network. And yet, here he was, an instant later.

He re-entered the lightrail, and once again found himself at another hub, light-years distant still.

His travel on the network was *instantaneous*.

But the ability to travel at great speed wasn't something entirely new to him. The Current could do this on the planet.

Here, however, was another opportunity. If Edward was right, there were answers here.

This time, as he entered the stream of the lightrail, he did not submerge completely, but instead reached in with a part of himself. He spread himself wide, trying to fill the whole space as he had back on the colony, when he'd absorbed all of the First Colony waveforms.

Suddenly he was *everywhere*. Any part of space touched by the lightrail was now his "location," and he could feel and see and hear and taste and touch *everything*.

He could sense the lightrail hubs and relays. But more important, he could sense the ships. They moved along at, admittedly, a good pace, though it was a snail's pace compared to how Edward moved.

For the first time, however, he could see how the whole system worked. He could see how *inefficient* it was.

On a whim, he reached out and "nudged" one of the ships. It picked up speed instantly, and moved to the next lightrail hub in a few minutes, where it would have taken days.

It was far from being the instantaneous leap that Edward could make, but it was significantly faster than anything these vessels had done before. If they were made of energy, Edward could move them from point A to point B in the space of a thought.

All that considered, it was another discovery that mattered most to him. As he pulsed throughout the lightrail, touching every part of it at once, he began to sense the presence of *others*.

They came slowly at first, but their progress was inevitable. First a dozen or so, then a few hundred. Before long, thousands. *Thousands* of souls, dancing in the pulse of the lightrail network, awakening, emerging, becoming unique and whole and *free*.

He had been right.

He could hear them, in his mind. With each passing second they became a bit louder, a bit more independent. They each became one among many.

Edward wasn't immune to the changes, either. He could feel a sort of fog lift from his mind. He could think clearer, and understand more readily. His mind acted spongelike, taking in all new information and data, filtering it, assigning relevance, in a way he'd never been capable of in his life before.

He became aware of the patterns. With his new perception, when he chose, he could listen in, hearing ship communications transmitted over a vessel's internal wiring and broadcast from speakers mounted in walls or in control panels or on desktops.

He couldn't just peek inside the pure data. It didn't work that way. With all of his abilities, he was still subject to the limitations of his own senses. But they were enough. Especially now that he was practically everywhere at once. He might not understand the pure data, but he could hear and see its outcome as it was heard by humans.

That was how he discovered the message.

He heard the message as snippets, played by crew members on a myriad of vessels. It took some time to realize that the vessels were all Esool. And the message, in every case, started the same way —

"This is Admiral Norchek. We are all in grave danger. Any vessel within range should immediately make heading to the attached coordinates."

The message continued, with a description of events happening on Earth. When Edward had heard it all, he knew he had to act, and fast. Everything depended on it. The Current had only just become a race of its own, but if he did not act immediately it would not exist by the end of the day.

Leaving the others to move and grow amid the flow of the lightrail, Edward decided to be back at the shuttle, and in that instant he was.

They were celebrating again. They had just connected to someone from Earth, and transferred him to the surface to speak with Somar. Edward had no time to waste, and immediately began exercising some influence over the shuttles controls.

They panicked, and tried to figure out what was happening. Alan, too late, realized what it was. "It's him," he said.

No time, Edward thought. *There's no time. He will stop me if he can.*

Before that could happen, Edward activated the shuttles engines, and moved them all into the lightrail. An instant later they were moving faster than any vessel had ever moved in the history of humanity or the Esool.

Edward prayed it would be fast enough.

THE FIRST FEW **hours after waking are the hungriest.** The Chairman had a standing order for breakfast to be served as soon as he emerged from his "safe room," though there was never any forewarning of when that would be. The staff were all made aware that he was emerging from stasis only when he was fully awake and dressed. As the safe room rose from its secured location, the staff would frantically run about, making ready.

He had not yet been able to catch them unprepared, though he so enjoyed the challenge.

Breakfast was what most might refer to as "hearty." Meats, both authentic and artificial, were piled on numerous large platters. Eggs from real chickens (though there hadn't been a "real" chicken since the GMO crisis in 2028), prepared in four different ways, were arranged at hand. Breads of every description were piled in rafts. Syrups, sauces, and gravies filled numerous carafes. Coffee was at the ready, his cup always filled, always hot.

Consuming this breakfast took the better part of an hour, and while he did so he watched a recap of current events on a display rising from the end of the table. The news was almost always the same. A celebrity did something untoward to someone. The impoverished were in revolt in some backwater area of Earth. Death count was rising after the collapse of some building in some ghetto in some over-crowded city. Savages ruled the news.

There was very little mention of the missing colonists from the Citadel vessel. This was, of course, to be expected. The ECF would hardly want it to be common knowledge that a colony vessel had simply *vanished* from the lightrail network.

Of course, the presence — or rather the *absence* — of some very well-known individuals made it nearly impossible to keep things entirely under wraps. That fool manager of Corey's had leaked the story of the A-lister boarding a shuttle for Citadel. Taggart's own people had refused to comment, which was as much as making a statement that he was confirmed missing. Damn fools, all of them.

With his meal complete, the Chairman rose and made his way to his home office. The environment adjusted to his presence. Lights brightened. The temperature rapidly changed to what the Chairman felt was comfortable. The various security precautions disengaged and re-engaged as he passed.

Within his office he took a seat. A light was already blinking on his desktop, indicating an incoming call. He swiped the screen and Rudford's face appeared.

"I trust all is well," the Chairman said.

Rudford nodded. "Of course, sir. The activation protocol for the kill switch is in your personal data folder. Per your request, it is completely isolated from other systems. Only you can access it."

The Chairman brought up the protocol. A simple measure for something so vast in consequences. At his command, he would control the fate of of every human in the universe. Not to mention the *shrubs*. For the humans, he felt a sort of pity, tempered with his belief that they deserved what they got for leaving the home world behind. For the latter, he felt an elation of sorts. To be rid of them, once and for all. To strike them at their core. To eliminate the vermin who threatened to corrupt the nobility of humanity, of Earth. The Chairman smiled.

The effect on Rudford was noticeable. The Chairman's

smile often caused others to shiver. It might be the slightly sharpened teeth. Or perhaps it was just the fact that the Chairman smiled so infrequently, and usually only when he was trying to make a point.

"I am preparing to leave Taggart Prime and return to Earth," Rudford said. "If you will permit me to return before using the kill switch, of course."

"Of course," the Chairman said. "And what of O'Neill?"

"He will suffer an unfortunate accident in approximately one hour."

"So soon?" the Chairman asked. "You have grown impatient, I see."

Rudford nodded. "I find him bothersome."

The Chairman chuckled. "Very well, Rudford. I do understand. Cleaning house, and all that."

"When will you use the kill switch?" Rudford asked.

"Oh, I'm not entirely certain. Perhaps if I become irritated with someone who has become *bothersome*."

Rudford's change in expression only registered for an instant before his resolve and composure reasserted themselves. The Chairman chuckled again. "You have nothing to fear, Rudford. Return home, shake the dust of that forsaken moon from your heels, and together we will enjoy a universe devoid of star travel and the Esool."

Rudford nodded. "Very well, sir. I look forward to—"

The screen went dark.

In truth, *everything* went dark. The lights, the display, the faux scenery from the window — the entire grid was offline.

This was not possible. The Chairman's home could not *be* offline. And, because it was impossible, the Chairman was fully aware of what was happening.

He sprang to his feet just as the doors of his office burst open with concussive force that would have knocked anyone else to their knees. Men in nondescript uniforms, bearing MD guns, rushed into the room amid a cloud of dust and debris from the small explosives they had used.

They trained their weapons on him.

Without hesitation, the Chairman crouched behind his desk just as they were firing. The desk would not withstand multiple hits from MD fire, but it bought him enough time to open the panel in the floor and slip inside.

He pulled the panel back into place, engaging the deadlocks, and then made his way as quickly as possible to the secondary entrance of his safe room.

Too late he remembered the kill switch protocol. It was encrypted and stored in his personal data folder. No one but him could get to it. But that folder was tied specifically to his desk, and that was currently a smoldering ruin. Even if he gained access to the desk again, he would never be able to activate the kill switch.

But he had *another* desk.

He rushed into the safe room, engaged its security protocols, and rode in it like an elevator until he reached a private garage, with an automated limousine waiting, repulsor drive running.

The driver was one of the regular rotation. He was well-trained, in far more than driving. He served as a bodyguard and an assassin at need. "I must reach my office at Earth First headquarters. Damn the flight speed laws."

"Yes, sir," the man said.

In seconds they were flying through the exit tunnel, winding their way out of the mountain, exiting miles from the Chairman's home. Moments later they were in the air and moving at speeds that were beyond illegal.

As they flew, the Chairman made several calls, ensuring that security was on high alert at the Earth First headquarters. He would arrive at one of the undisclosed entry points, and it was absolute priority that he be ushered to his office with no delay.

Calls and plans made, the Chairman settled into his seat. It would be a while before they arrived, even at this great speed. In that time, the invaders were sure to determine that he was no longer in his home, and they would certainly ascertain where he was going. Judging by the response from his people at Earth First, they had not yet made the same play on the offices as they had in his home.

There was still time.

"Oh," the Chairman said, suddenly remembering, delighted. He reached forward and called up the security protocols for his home. With quick swipes he initiated full defensive protocols. The house may have been powered down, but the mountain — that was a different story. And the explosive charges underlying the foundations of his home were on the mountain's power grid for that very reason.

It seemed there wasn't much time after all. Depending on where you were standing.

"MOVE! MOVE! MOVE!" Foster shouted to his men as he and Norchek ran for the shuttles, explosions toppling the mansion and a large chunk of the mountain in their wake. They had dropped in from orbit, at high speed, to help avoid detection as their EM pulse took out the Chairman's power grid and internal defenses. But there would be no avoiding the detection of this level of destruction.

They launched even as the ground under their feet crumbled away. Smoke and dust were already rolling in great waves, covering everything in a powdery ash. The noise was deafening.

When they were in the air, Foster called for a head count.

"Three casualties, sir," one of the men reported. "Two humans and one Esool."

Norchek felt a momentary spike of grief over the loss of these men, human and Esool alike. The humans had all volunteered, once Foster had explained what was happening. "My renegades," Foster called them.

They could not trust the ECF to respond in time, if at all. The corruption of Earth First ran too deep into the organization. Foster's men, however, were loyal to Foster. And, by his own admission, to money. "They'll expect to be paid," Foster said.

Norchek had agreed, and would ensure that they were somehow compensated. Including the families of the dead.

The shuttles shot skyward, edging closer to the atmosphere's edge. By now they would certainly have been noticed. "What reaction can we expect from the ECF?" Norchek asked.

"They're not going to be happy."

Norchek nodded. "I worry for the treaty."

"Don't," Foster said. "Worry more about the court marshal. We're operating illegally on Earth soil. They'll take that pretty serious."

"I will gladly accept responsibility and whatever punishment the ECF and my people deem necessary, but I would prefer to end this threat to the lightrail before that happens."

Foster nodded. "Well, we're operating in the black as much as possible. My contacts back at ECF headquarters will do everything they can to mask our presence in the shuttles. Nothing they can do to hide the destruction of a mountain, though." He checked a display in front of him. "Media is already in full chatter mode. I think we might get lucky, getting away as fast as we did."

"The bodies of our fallen?" Norchek asked.

"Recovered," Foster said, glancing at information streaming in. He looked up, "We may have missed the Chairman, but at least we got his system. It's deadlocked, but maybe we can hack it."

"I do not believe that will be the case," Norchek said. "It is clear the Chairman is a resourceful man operating under a deep paranoia. His home was fortified better than many military installations. I believe that whatever is stored in his system will be beyond our reach."

"Maybe so," Foster said. "But he's headed straight to the Earth First facility. I think he has a backup."

"Then we must find it and destroy it as well."

The three shuttles roared through the sky toward Earth First. All attention, according the media, seemed to be on the Rocky Mountains. Stray chatter on the comms indicated that the ECF was paying close attention, in case this was some form of terrorist attack. Foster's people at ECF headquarters had managed, so far, to mask their shuttle traffic by making them appear to be responders on their *way* to the mountain, rather than leaving it.

"Very clever," Norchek said.

"For however long it lasts. If we don't put down soon someone is going to look over a shoulder or check data for themselves and the whole thing will crumble."

There was a chime from comms and Foster answered. One of his men, dressed in the nondescript, dark military uniform they all wore, appeared onscreen. "Sir, we will touch down in about forty minutes. We may have a problem. Scans indicate a couple of ECF shuttles already at the facility."

"Ours?" Foster asked.

"What do you think?"

Foster cursed. "DeCarte," he said. "This may get bad."

"If they delay us," Norchek said, "It will give the Chairman enough time to activate the kill switch."

"Sir," the man onscreen said. "One of the techs has been studying the Chairman's system. He can't crack it, but he found something interesting. There's a communications protocol installed, surface level. It's part of the baseline code, actually. The tech says it's 'vanity code,' from Taggart industries."

"What's it for?" Foster asked.

"Turns out it was letting the Chairman talk to someone off world."

"In orbit?" Foster asked.

The man shook his head. "No, sir, on a moon in the lightrail network."

Foster and Norchek exchanged stunned looks. Norchek turned back to the screen, "You are saying that the Chairman possesses technology that allows him to communicate instantly with someone lightyears away?"

"I'm saying we all do," he said. "This protocol is already installed in every Taggart Industries system. It just has to be activated. Our tech was able to reverse engineer the protocol, based on the data buffer. It's actually not all that difficult, once you know it's there. Once it's activated on one side of comms it automatically turns on for any system you communicate with. Something to do with 'sympathetic particles.' It's a little beyond me."

"But we can use this technology to communicate with distant worlds? Distant vessels?" Norchek asked.

"Yes, sir."

"Transmit the protocols immediately," Norchek said.

"What do you have in mind?" Foster asked.

Norchek was already receiving the protocols, and engaging them on the shuttle's comms. "If we are unable to breach the Chairman's defenses, perhaps we can reach the kill switch itself. I am sending a message to my people, with the coordinates of that moon."

"Is anyone close enough to get there in time?"

Norchek shook his head. "I do not know. The moon's coordinates put it in an area of the network that is not frequented by my people."

Foster checked the coordinates. "Or anyone," he said. "It's pretty remote."

"It is a measure of hope," Norchek said. He opened a communications channel, setting it as a blanket broadcast to all Esool vessels, in the same fashion he would use with vessels in orbit. "This is Admiral Norchek of the Esool. I am speaking to you from Earth, using a newly discovered communications protocol. One of my men will send you all the information we have on this system. However, there is a matter of some urgency. I am transmitting coordinates to a moon designated Taggart Prime, as well as all of the data we posses on a device meant to disable the lightrail network.

"I am calling for all Esool vessels to divert to Taggart Prime immediately. You must find and destroy this kill switch before it can be activated. We are attempting to block its use from Earth, but our progress is impeded. Our only hope may be to reach that moon. You have your orders. Nolad's blessings to you all."

He closed the channel. Everyone in the shuttle was silent. Norchek had not realized how much chatter had been happening around him all this while, but now the silence was palpable.

It was possible these men had not known the severe consequences of losing this battle. No matter. They were beyond the need or the use of secrecy.

Norchek busied himself with studying the layout of the Earth First facility, discussing strategies and approaches with Foster and his men. There was a growing tension in the room as everyone struggled to remain patient. Even the Esool seemed on edge. Norchek understood their anxiety. Losing this battle would mean never returning to the Esool home world. It would mean losing everyone they cared about. It might also mean their execution, if the ECF chose to see Norchek's mission as the cause of these events. Much was at stake, however, beyond the personal freedoms or even the lives of Norchek and these men. The fate of two races depended on their actions today.

Finally the comms chimed and Foster's man appeared onscreen "Sir, we're on the ground in five."

Foster stood, hefting his MD rifle. "Suit up, ladies and gentlemen. We're going in hot."

CHAPTER 11

THE LIGHT FADED, REPLACED BY BLACK. MITCH, REILLY, AND Alan found themselves staring in bewilderment at each other, frozen in a moment, unsure if they should even move.

"What just happened?" Mitch asked.

Reilly and Alan came back to life, checking displays for data.

"We're ... not where we started," Alan said.

"Where the hell *are* we?" Mitch shouted.

"I think we're orbiting Taggart Prime," Alan said quietly.

Reilly, dumfounded, checked her own display. "He's right," she said. She looked up at them. "Did we go into stasis when I wasn't looking? Or did we just make a three month journey in, like, thirty seconds?"

Mitch shook his head. "This doesn't make sense."

"It was Edward," Alan said.

Mitch and Reilly looked at him.

"Before we left, he was talking about making contact with the lightrail." Alan explained everything he knew, starting with Edward absorbing the First Colony personalities and his discovery that "being everywhere" could make it possible to separate individual personalities from the Current.

"And he thinks the lightrail will help him do that?" Reilly asked.

"The Current is an energy life form. The lightrail contains enough energy to help it manifest every one of those waveforms. It could work," Alan said.

"It did work," a voice said from the crew chamber doorway.

They all looked to see Edward, framed by a soft light from the porthole in the door.

"Edward," Alan said.

"It worked," he said. "They're out there. They're everywhere."

Mitch stood. He could feel tension in his shoulders, in his jaw. "What did you do?" he asked.

Edward stepped forward and Mitch tensed, ready for anything. Edward stopped. "I'm not going to harm anyone," he said softly.

"I'm not so sure about that!" Mitch said. "We're orbiting a moon three months away from the colony, and we got here in *seconds*. You've infected the lightrail with thousands of personalities. You have no idea what might happen because of that!"

"No," Edward said. "I don't. Neither do you. But for the moment there are thousands of souls alive and growing there. They have a chance. They never would have had it if I hadn't brought them here. That's worth any risk."

"To who!" Mitch roared. Reilly stepped close to him, put a hand on his arm, and he felt himself calm a bit, instantly.

"To us," Edward said. "To our species."

Mitch started to say something, but stopped. He blinked.

He inhaled and exhaled. "It's done," he said. "We're here now."

"Why *are* we here?" Alan asked.

Edward looked at him, and Mitch noticed that his actions were much more *human* than before. He was more *present*, not staring off into the distance.

"It's all in jeopardy," Edward said. "There is an Admiral, an Esool named Norchek. He sent an order over the lightrail, using Taggart's protocol. He's asked all Esool come here, to find and destroy the kill switch."

"The kill switch?" Mitch asked. "Taggart's lightrail kill switch? How would he even know about it?"

"Earth First has learned of it. Someone called the Chairman."

They looked at each other, and finally Mitch said. "This Chairman is planning to shut down the lightrail? It makes sense. Earth First has tried things like this before."

"They tried to stop all of this before it even started," Alan said. "By destroying First Colony."

"And now they may actually do it," Reilly said.

"No!" Edward said, and Mitch was surprised by his emotion. He had definitely changed. Somehow, by becoming an individual, Edward had become more than he had been before.

"What can we do?" Mitch asked.

"Go to the surface and find the kill switch. I'm not sure I can find it, on my own. I only know what I was able to overhear, on thousands of lightrail ships. You and Alan might be able to find it faster, to destroy it."

Mitch nodded. He looked at Reilly. "Take us down."

She rushed to the controls, linking in quickly.

Alan checked one of the displays, bringing up scans of the surface. "The most likely place is probably that large facility on the southern continent. It has its own direct link to the orbital relay. I'm transferring coordinates."

"Got it," Reilly said, and pushed the shuttle into motion, aiming at the planet's surface.

Mitch turned to Edward. "We have a few minutes. How did you do this? How did you get us here?"

Edward was silent for a moment, then said, "I can't say for sure, but somehow I can push things along on the lightrail. Not quite at the same speed I can travel, but fast. Really fast."

"I'll say," Mitch said. "I'm going to want to know how you did it, when this is all over. Something like that could eliminate the need for stasis. It could make it possible to move around among the colonies in days instead of months and years. That's going to change everything."

"It already has," Edward said. "And I promise, if we can save the lightrail and my people today, there are no secrets. I will help you figure out how to make this work."

Mitch nodded. He couldn't help catching that small statement, however. *My people*, Edward had said. Not human, but Current.

How long would the Current's interests coincide with those of humanity? Or the Esool? Fifty years of war with the Esool had not quite been forgotten by humanity. What would happen with an entirely new species in the mix? One that could literally control the lightrail, and the fate of the other two?

No time for that now. Whatever problems might be on the horizon, with the Current or with Earth First or anyone else, they would have to be dealt with later.

"We're touching down in a minute," Reilly announced.

True enough, a moment later they felt the slight jolt of the shuttle making contact with the surface.

Alan stood, and Reilly extricated herself from the controls. They all stood, looking at Mitch. "Now what?" Reilly asked.

"Good question. We don't have any weapons. Those are all back on the colony."

Reilly turned and rifled through a tool box under the pilot's station. "I have this," she said, hefting a large wrench that had seen better days. It was scorched and melted.

"Isn't that mine?" Mitch asked.

"It comes in handy for smacking energy-based life-forms," she said, smiling at Edward. "Maybe it will work on the old fashioned solid kind, too."

Mitch and Alan followed suit, grabbing whatever they could find. Mitch found a wrench of his own. Alan retrieved a long piece of metal conduit from a bin that held spare parts. They were armed, and maybe even ready.

"What about you?" Reilly asked Edward.

"I have my own ways," Edward said.

"Right," Reilly said, stroking the melted ripples of the wrench.

"Ok," Mitch said. "Time to move out."

———

ALAN WAS FOCUSED on the handheld, which wasn't easy. Mitch was hovering.

"You're sure you've got this?" he asked.

"I'm sure."

"If you don't have this we'll set off alarms all over this place. There's no telling what kind of security they have. You're sure?"

Without looking up, Alan said, "I made an entire colony vessel disappear from the lightrail, and before that I kept a man hidden in stasis for over a hundred years while I slept in a stasis pod under him. I got this."

"Right," Mitch said. "All that you just said, I forgot about that."

"Can we get this moving a little faster?" Reilly said, hefting her wrench and eyeing the area around them, on the lookout for anyone who came along.

"All those things I said? I didn't have two people chattering in my ear at the time."

"Look who's touchy," Reilly said.

"Must be all the time travel."

Alan said nothing, and made no expression, but he felt like smiling. Banter was good. Banter meant he might be forgiven.

Edward leaned in. "I could phase through the door and open it from the inside."

Alan stopped what he was doing and looked up. Everyone was looking at Edward, who surprisingly looked a little uncomfortable. "I sort of forgot."

"It won't work anyway," Alan said, getting back to work. "This door is deadlocked if the power shuts down, and unless you know the code you couldn't open it."

"But you've got this," Mitch said.

Just then there was an audible click as deadlock tumblers rotated up and out of the way. Alan reached and touched the door's control panel, and it slid open quietly. "I got this," Alan said, walking through the door and into the facility.

"Don't get cocky," Mitch said, though he was struggling to keep his face straight.

They entered a large chamber, a sort of foyer where workers might pull on safety equipment or pick up and drop off small equipment. On the far wall was another door, no lock in sight. On either side of that were two banks of controls and monitors, part of the facility's power system. They made their way to the door.

"Edward," Mitch said, "can you maybe go invisible, like you did before? Move around and get some information, so we're not going in blind?"

"Yes," Edward said, and promptly disappeared.

Reilly jumped. "I hate that!" she said to thin air.

"What about us?" Alan asked.

Mitch looked around, then walked to one of the instrument panels. He inspected it, swiping through a few pages of information streaming in from the facility. "This places uses a *lot* of power," he said.

"It's sustaining a constant link to the lightrail," Alan said, checking his handheld.

"What do you mean?" Reilly asked. "You mean, here on the *planet?*"

"Moon," Alan corrected. "And yeah. I think you could actually make a lightrail jump right from this building."

"That's illegal," Reilly said.

"I don't think Taggart cared at the time," Mitch said.

"It's not as cut and dry as that anyway. I don't think this link was meant for travel. I think it's a power supply."

"So the power isn't being used to keep the link open. It's being drawn from the lightrail itself?"

Alan nodded. "Pretty cool, actually."

Mitch looked to each of them. "Taggart really was serious about all this. He was going to shut down the lightrail."

"Temporarily," Alan said. "His plan was to control it."

"Well, isn't that nice of him," Mitch said, a sour expression on his face.

"Does this change anything for us?" Reilly asked.

Alan shrugged. "I don't think so. We'll know later, I'm guessing."

"Let's get moving," Mitch said. "Edward can find us. But I have a feeling that time isn't on our side."

They stepped through the door and into the facility proper. Alan hadn't seen anything like this since before going into stasis. It resembled one of the large power plants his father had taken him to as a kid. Knots and gnarls of metal twisted upward and outward like tree roots, penetrating into walls, ceiling, and floor. It was a massive operation.

"What is this place *for*?" Reilly asked.

Alan considered. "I think Taggart was going to use this place to prime the lightrail, to restart it after it was shut off."

"So you're saying that if the Chairman activates the kill switch we can restart the lightrail from here?" Mitch asked.

"Maybe, but I don't know if I'd risk it," Alan said. "Whatever the Chairman's man has done here, he might have rigged the place to self destruct after he was gone. They don't need a primer for the lightrail. Their goal is to shut the whole thing down permanently."

"That makes sense," Mitch said as he stared up into the twists and turns of metal above.

Alan consulted the handheld. "This way," he said, nodding. "I have a schematic of the place. Should help us move around."

"Does it have a big X where the kill switch will be?" Reilly asked.

Alan shook his head. "No, sorry," he said.

"Kidding," Reilly said.

They walked on, turning down several corridors, going deeper into the facility until even Alan wasn't sure if the handheld and the map would be enough to get them back out. "There's a central room that I think may be a control room. That seems the most likely place. It's up ahead."

"Where *is* everyone?" Reilly said.

"I think the whole facility is automated," Mitch said. "Makes sense. Taggart couldn't trust anyone when it came to shutting down the lightrail, even temporarily. Someone was bound to have a problem with it."

They came to an large door. This one had another security access panel. Alan stepped forward and studied it, then reached out and touched the screen. The large door slid aside.

Mitch and Reilly stared at him.

"It was unlocked," he said.

"Which means we're probably not alone here," Mitch said.

They entered the room.

The room was crammed with machinery and equipment. Control panels flickered with cascades of data, undulating graphs and meters could be seen on every display.

On the floor before one terminal a man lay still, face down. Blood and bits of something unpleasant looking made a spray pattern on the floor, walls, and equipment that would have been behind him.

Mitch and Alan crouched beside him. Alan could see a wound at the base of his skull. Mitch reached out, cautiously, and lifted the man's head, peering at his face and neck. "No entry wound," Mitch said.

Alan looked at his handheld. "There's a swarm of nanobots where his *medulla oblongata* used to be. It looks like they detonated."

There was a muffled sound and a small squeak from behind them, and Mitch and Alan turned to find Reilly being held in a choke hold by a man wielding a MD handgun. They were on their feet in seconds, and Alan put a hand on Mitch's arm to keep him from leaping at the man.

"There, there," the man said. "No need for this poor girl to end up like Mr. O'Neill there," he said, nodding to the body. "I assume the three of you are working with Taggart."

Alan wasn't sure how to answer, or what to do. Reilly, on the other hand, wasn't so limited.

In a burst she twisted, gaining enough leverage to spring upward from the floor and slam the back of her head into the man's nose before jerking forward, breaking free of his grip as he reacted in surprise.

He fired, and Reilly cried out before falling to the floor.

"Reilly!" Mitch yelled.

To Alan's surprise, Mitch leapt past her and directly to the man with the gun. He swung his wrench and made hard, bone-crunching contact with the man's wrist. The gun flew, sliding a foot or so away on the floor. Mitch had the man on the ground and was laying into him with swift punches, the wrench clutched tightly in his fist all the while.

Alan dropped to Reilly's side to check on her. She lifted herself to her knees, a hand on the back of her neck. Alan looked at the wound, and was relieved to see she'd only been grazed. The wound was completely cauterized. She'd have a scar, but not even a very bad one. She was ok.

He turned and was planning to help Mitch when the man suddenly managed to grab Mitch and fling him to one side. He made a sort of flipping motion, and was instantly on his feet, then did a shoulder roll to the MD gun, picking it up in his good hand and training it on them before anyone could react.

He was highly trained, and knew how to kill. Alan stepped back, trying to put himself between the gunman and Reilly, to give her some sort of chance, even though he knew the MD disk would pass through him like he wasn't there. Instead of firing on them, however, he slowly moved the gun from Alan to Mitch and back again. "Gather up," he said.

Mitch limped over to Alan. The two of them made a wall between the man and Reilly, who was still on the floor behind them.

"You too, dear," the man said, making a show of peering around them. "I want to see everyone."

Reilly stood and stepped between Mitch and Alan.

"Good," the man said. "Now, as I was saying, you must be working with Taggart. My employer would be very interested in knowing where Taggart has gotten himself. It would be good to have him completely out of the way, and I assume that he survived the attempt on his life."

"You mean the attempt to blow up Citadel and kill thousands of innocent people just to get to one man?" Mitch sneered.

"Technically two people," the man smiled. "Corey was on that vessel as well, wasn't he? At any rate, I'm guessing it didn't work. So where is he?"

"He's here," Alan said. He could feel the others react, wanting to glance at him, but they kept their eyes on the man. Alan didn't.

"I seriously doubt he is on this moon," the man said. "I would have found him by now."

Alan smiled.

"Well, you seem awfully amused. Are you trying to tell me Taggart somehow hid out on this moon, avoiding intensive scans for weeks? Highly unlikely. And there are no vessels in orbit."

"No," Alan said. "But I wasn't talking about Taggart." He turned his head and saw Mitch smile as well.

The man was nervous, and while keeping his gun trained on them he turned his body slightly and glanced over his shoulder.

On the opposite end of the room, Edward stood, watching.

The man reacted quickly, turning the MD gun on Edward and firing several disks into him. They passed through with no effect.

In a blink, however, Edward was standing inches away from the barrel of the gun.

The man let out an involuntary cry, and fired several more rounds, all to no effect.

Edward looked at the man curiously, as if staring *into* him. In a flash he reached out, his hand passing into the man's head as if it wasn't there. Again the man cried out, but was suddenly silenced by a small explosion at the base of his skull. It was contained by a small EM field that, seconds before, had formed an invisible dome around the man's head.

The man fell away, slumping to the floor in a heap. Dead.

They all looked at Edward. Alan wasn't sure what to say, or even how he felt about what just happened. Before they can truly react, Edward says, "I've found the kill switch."

"Yeah," Mitch said quietly, looking at the man.

"The kill switch for the lightrail. This way," Edward said, and they rushed to follow him.

They ran through an irregular opening in the wall at the end of the room, a melted pile of slag that formed hardening puddles on either side of what was once a door. Edward's handiwork, Alan realized. An open door for them to gain access to the chamber beyond.

The room was fairly plain. A single system dominated

all of one wall. Alan rushed to it, and used his handheld to start scanning and making intrusions. "I think I can backdoor in using Taggart's protocol. It might take a while." He started tapping frantically at the screen, running into wall after wall, defeating security protocols at the cost of time.

"Can't Edward just fry it?" Mitch asked, impatient.

"I have no idea what that would do. There might be a failsafe. We might take the lightrail out ourselves."

Mitch said nothing.

"What can we do?" Reilly asked quietly. She was talking to Mitch, but Alan could hear her the sound of helplessness and fear in her voice.

"Nothing," Mitch said. "This is up to Alan now. He's got this."

Alan didn't react, but wanted to. Hearing the confidence that Mitch had in him made everything come into focus. It was like breathing again after holding his breath for a long time.

And then he saw it.

A few passes, a few feints and dodges, and then a decisive attack. The walls came down. The ports opened.

He was in.

He found the protocols for the kill switch and locked them. He swept it clean, removing every trace of it from Taggart's system.

He looked up to see everyone, even Edward, staring at him expectantly.

"I did it," he said.

Mitch and Reilly cheered, rushing forward and grabbing him, squeezing him between them in a hug hard enough to crush ribs. They were whooping and cheering and jumping up and down.

Minutes later, as the excitement died down, Mitch turned to Edward, who also seemed pretty pleased.

"Ok, mission accomplished. Universe saved. And nothing crucial blew up, so that's different. What's next?"

"Now," Edward said, "I take you back to the colony."

"Home," Reilly said, scooting in beside Mitch. She looked back and held a hand out to Alan, and pulled him into a side hug as well. "You take us home."

FROM THE MOMENT **they landed they took heavy fire.** Norchek led a charge of Esool and human operatives through corridors guarded by ECF officers. Most wore the blue uniforms of the ECF, and bore insignia showing their rank and even their names.

"DeCarte must have been forced to grab every non-com he could find. Everyone in his network," Foster said as they crouched for cover. He smiled at Norchek.

"I fail to see why this should amuse you," Norchek said.

"Your peace treaty, Admiral. This pretty much guarantees it's safe. The ECF is going to do everything it can to cover this up."

Norchek nodded, feeling a sense of relief. Foster was right. The ECF would be forced to hide this incursion. In all likelihood they would blame the explosion in Colorado on Earth First, and claim that this was a raid on their headquarters. The truth would be buried, but the result would coincide with Norchek's goals.

They continued their push deeper into the facility. Norchek was greatly concerned over the amount of time it was taking. Surely the Chairman had reached his office by now, had gained access to his private systems, had activated the kill switch. Their only hope now, as Norchek saw it, was to recover the Chairman and his system, and force the man to give them access so they could undo the damage.

Foster's men were more efficient at the business of close-quarter combat than their enemies. DeCarte's men were primarily trained for intelligence gathering and systems operations. They had the advantage of numbers, but their tactics were flawed. In time, Foster was able to overcome their advantage with several well-placed maneuvers.

In short measure they found themselves in front of the Chairman's office. Foster had one of his men place charges, and in seconds the door disintegrated in splinters and they rushed inside. The sounds of gunfire and men yelling "Down! Down! Down!" could be heard even from Norchek's position. As things settled and quieted, Norchek led his small team in through the door, weapons ready.

The room was now secure.

To Norchek's surprise, the Chairman was sitting peace-fully behind his desk.

Tendrils of smoke curled through shafts of light from the ceiling. Debris from the door had not quite made it to the far wall of the room — it formed a valley of destruction that ended with the perfect order of the Chairman's desk. A large display on the wall behind him showed an inviting forest scene that reminded Norchek of home.

The Chairman had a small wooden box in front of him. Its lid was open, revealing a cluster of small candies wrapped in yellow plastic. The Chairman sat, twisting an empty wrapper between his fingers, and sucking on one of the candies. He did not meet anyone's gaze, but stared at the wrapper. Finally he spoke.

"The device did not work," he said simply. His tone had a note of amusement.

This is a game to him, Norchek realized. *He realizes he has lost, but he will not capitulate. Not so easily.*

"Pity," the Chairman said. He let the wrapper fall away and lowered his hands to the surface of the desk. "But that was always a possibility. I gambled everything on this move, and lost. I do so hate losing."

With that the Chairman rose quickly from his chair, faster than Norchek would have believed for someone his size. He grabbed the edge of the desk, and with very little effort he hoisted it up and rushed forward, using the massive desk as a shield and battering ram.

Two of Norchek's men were knocked aside, and the Chairman fairly flung the desk toward Norchek and the other soldiers, forcing them to leap out of its way. In a burst of speed the Chairman reached with one huge hand and grabbed one solider by the neck, snapping it easily.

Foster leapt in front of Norchek, to protect him, and the Chairman grabbed him by the face, twisting and lifting him until his feet dangled, kicking uselessly.

Norchek, weapon drawn, leapt toward the Chairman, firing when his line of sight was clear. The remaining Esool and humans did the same, firing multiple rounds into the Chairman's massive body. After a few seconds the mountainous man finally staggered back, dropping Foster to the ground. He clutched at Norchek — a look of disgusted anger coloring his features. Finally, with a slight gasp, he smiled at Norcheck, baring his teeth as if preparing to lunge and bite. And then all was quiet. He staggered once, and then crumpled slowly to the floor, dead.

Norchek crouched to help Foster to his feet. "Are you injured?" he asked.

Foster shook his head. "No. I'm good," he said, though he was gasping for breath. "Thank you."

Norchek nodded.

They both stood and stared down at the Chairman's body.

"He said it didn't work," Foster huffed. "The kill switch? Did your people get to it in time?"

Norchek shook his head. "I do not believe that is possible."

"Something was possible," Foster said. "He was pretty certain. And pretty pissed." He said this last while rubbing his neck.

"Sir!" They looked to see the comms officer rushing towed them. "Our people back at ECF headquarters are reporting that the Citadel colony has been located! They're alive!"

Norchek felt a wave of relief. "And Somar?" he asked.

The man nodded. "Yes, sir," he said. "He's alive. There were casualties, but there are thousands of survivors. They're alive. They're on a colony world. They're using the communication protocols from Taggart's technology."

Foster whooped, and his men joined him. They cheered and celebrated. Even Norchek's men were smiling, though the Esool were far more reserved than the humans in their exuberance.

They had done it. At the risk of everything, they had stopped the plans of this madman. There were still many questions to be answered, but for the moment Norchek and his men were content with their victory.

He gave orders to secure the rest of the facility, and made his way to one of the shuttles. He would use the new communication protocol to speak to Somar again. It would be good to hear his voice.

CHAPTER 12

FLASH.

The shuttle appeared in orbit above the Citadel colony world, and Mitch marveled at the speed with which they had just crossed the expanse of space. No stasis. No sleeping through the journey. Just initiating a jump, and moments later arriving at your destination.

"It's not quite as fast as *we* can move along the lightrail," Edward explained.

"When you say 'we,' you mean the Current?" Alan asked.

"Yes," Edward said.

The Current. Mitch wasn't sure how he felt about the presence of thousands of once human minds, now in bodies composed of pure energy, flitting around on the network humanity depended on for travel. The repercussions of what had happened here would take decades to work out. They had risked their lives to destroy the kill switch on Taggart Prime, but maybe that had been a bit hasty. Maybe they would one day need a way to shut the network down.

We're only a day into having a new species around, Mitch thought, *and I'm already thinking about war.*

Reilly dipped the shuttle into the planet's atmosphere and landed near Central Command.

Mitch was still surprised by the sight of the Citadel tower in ruins. It had stood so tall and proud, had been such a symbol of hope as they had all struggled. Now it was darkened by soot, and parts of it lay in twisted ruin nearby.

But it was still there. It still stood. And as they settled to the ground, Mitch realized it was more a symbol of hope than ever. The damage was severe, but could be repaired. And no one here would ever forget that it continued to stand, even when things were at their worst.

Moments later, the four of them were gathered in the Central Command building. Thomas and Somar were talking to Taggart, as well as with various engineers and Blue Collars.

"About time you folks showed up," Thomas said, smiling. "What took you?"

"Edward says that's as fast as he can push us without turning us into energy," Mitch said. "He's prone to excuses."

Thomas laughed, and pulled Mitch into a hug, followed by hugging Reilly and Alan. He hesitated with Edward.

"Go ahead," Edward said, sounding faux reluctant.

Thomas smiled and pulled him in for a big one.

"Tingly," Thomas said, stepping back with a grin on his face.

"I am not!" Edward said, and everyone, even Edward, laughed.

Laughed.

Mitch wondered if it was real, or some kind of simulation. He tried to shake this feeling, that Edward was somehow less than real. Certainly not *human*, but that didn't mean anything these days. He had saved them all, of course. But he'd also saved his own race. Whether he and the Current were truly friends to humanity, and to the Esool, remained to be seen.

They discussed the mission in detail.

Somar, seeming uncharacteristically unsteady and leaning on a table's edge, asked Edward, "What of the Current? You have succeeded in separating into individual personalities, within the lightrail?"

Edward nodded. "Yes. Each is becoming more distinct by the hour. In fact, they're requesting asylum."

Mitch blinked. "Asylum? Here?"

"For the moment, it's the only home they know."

"But don't they live in the lightrail now?" Reilly asked.

"They move in the lightrail, just as you do. It's a road, not a destination. They need time to exist independent of it."

"I believe that asylum can be arranged," Somar said. "Thomas and I have been in discussions with the ECF and Esool leadership. We have asked for official status as one of the colony worlds. Given your actions today, I believe that status will be granted without question."

"Plus there was some kind of dust up on Earth," Thomas said. "Something that's apparently a bit of a black eye for the ECF."

"I have spoken with Admiral Norchek, of the Esool," Somar said. "He assures me that we will receive whatever aid is necessary, and that the threat to the lightrail has been eliminated."

"Along with Earth First," Thomas said, looking directly at Alan.

"You're kidding," Alan said, eyes wide.

"They were apparently leading this entire thing," Thomas said. "Norchek's team discovered computer records linking them to everything. They contracted Eric Grayman to sabotage the Citadel colony vessel. They provided the explosives, and the order was to make sure no one survived. That alone would be enough for the ECF to take them down, but the attempt on the lightrail was over the top. Plus, they apparently blew up a mountain in Colorado, for some reason."

"So that's it?" Alan asked. "They're gone? For good?"

"For good," Thomas said, quietly. "And more importantly, Alan — they're to blame for this. Not you. All of this, all the deaths and all the damage, can be traced straight back to them. Understand?"

Alan nodded, though he didn't seem convinced. He would be, Mitch knew. In time.

Penny entered through one of the side doors, looking around frantically. She spotted Edward and rushed toward him, her hands in fists.

Alan stepped between them. "It's ok! It's ok!"

"You," she said to Edward, "are a *jerk!*"

"I know," Edward said sheepishly, tilting his head down.

Mitch couldn't help but smile as Alan, Penny, and Edward bickered. Edward was possibly the most powerful being in the universe, but Mitch was pretty sure Penny could take him. *That's what love does*, Mitch thought. *It gives you strength, and makes you volunteer to be weak.*

He glanced at Reilly, who was smiling at the three of them as well. She caught his look, and hooked her hand into his. It felt perfect there.

"If we can get back on track," Thomas said, and everyone settled down again. "There are ECF and Esool vessels inbound on the lightrail. Moving at normal speeds, apparently."

"We can speed them up, if you like," Edward said.

Thomas shook his head. "No. Not yet. Let's make the most of our time. Eventually we're going to have to work out when it's appropriate to give an assist on the lightrail. Or maybe figure out how you do what you do, and make it something the lightrail can do on its own."

"I have some thoughts on that," Alan said. "If Edward would be willing to do a few tests, I think I can figure out a way to modify the lightrail hubs permanently."

"You do that," Taggart said, "and I can guarantee that Taggart Industries will modify the entire network at no cost to the colonies. And you have a lifetime career with me."

Alan looked at him, nodding. Penny, maybe subconsciously, stepped closer to him and put a hand on the small of his back.

They looked good together, Mitch thought. They looked like they could work. Like they could be happy.

For the first time, Mitch realized that he had not only forgiven Alan, he actually *liked* him. All of his crimes, all of his sins, had been wiped clean with the events of the day. Just like that. Apparently even he couldn't hold a grudge forever.

"There's something else," Edward said, stepping forward and addressing Somar and Thomas directly. "Captain Alonzo."

Thomas and Somar exchanged glances. "What about him?"

"I can save him," Edward said. "By absorbing him into the Current."

The room was silent. Mitch felt a twisting in his gut. "How?" He asked. "He's not one of the waveforms. He's alive."

"True," Edward said. "But he's dying," he glanced at Thomas, who nodded.

"It's true. He's in deep stasis, and that's literally the only thing keeping him alive."

"If Alan uses what he knows to create a copy of his wave-form and mingle it with the interference wave, I can absorb him and take him into the lightrail, where he will become one of my people."

"Why would you do this?" Somar asked.

"I believe we need him," Edward said. "He is from this time, and understands humanity and the Esool, the politics and details of life today. He's a leader, and understands the ECF. He would know how to guide us, to prevent us from doing something wrong, or maybe destroying ourselves."

"He could act as an ambassador between your people and the ECF," Thomas said.

Edward nodded.

Somar said, "I am uncertain if this is wise. What you are proposing could have very serious repercussions. Giving new life to the First Colony personalities might be seen as a quirk of technology. They are duplicates of long-dead humans. But this ..."

"It would be like telling the colonies that it's possible to be immortal," Mitch said.

They looked at him, waiting. It was on their minds, too.

"Where's the line?" he asked. "How do you justify saving him, but not others?"

"I can't," Edward said. "And if you all agree, and tell me not to do it, I will understand. But I do believe he can help. I believe we need him."

They were quiet for a time, as each thought about what this meant. Mitch shook his head, but couldn't help thinking that he *wanted* Edward to save Alonzo. If it could be done, then he wanted it done.

It wasn't up to him, of course. But he could feel everyone looking at him.

"I think it has to be you," Thomas said. "You have to be the one to decide."

"Me?" Mitch asked. "Not even close, Thomas. That's a decision Somar has to make."

"It is not," Somar said. "I served only briefly with Captain Alonzo, though I knew him to be a good man. I cannot speak on behalf of humanity or the ECF, however. I can say that the Esool would see no injustice in this. We are accustomed to the concept of a transition from one form of life to another. Humanity may see this differently. You, more than any of us, are the most qualified to make this decision."

"Then we take it to the ECF," Mitch said. "I'm not qualified to decide on something like this."

Reilly squeezed his hand and said, "Mitch, you're the *only one* who's qualified. This isn't a chain of command decision. This is the Captain's life, and the choice only someone who knew him could make. He didn't have any family, other than his crew. You're it. You decide."

He felt her hand in his, and the strength that came from it. He looked around at all of the faces gathered, all looking at him, waiting. And he decided.

"Yes," he said, with no hesitancy in his voice. He turned to Edward, "Save him. But this can't be something you do. Not always. There's a reason people die, even when we don't want it."

Edward nodded. "I know. There's also a reason people live."

Mitch regarded him for a moment, then nodded.

"Well, that's fun," Thomas said. "I wonder if we'll be making any more universe-changing decisions today? There's still daylight left."

Everyone chuckled, though it was a dark humor. A lot had happened today, and no one, especially Mitch, was sure they were making the right decisions.

But that's what life is, he thought. *You make your decisions, right or wrong, and watch the world change. And you hope, on the whole, that the change is good.*

He had a hunch it would be.

EPILOGUE

THE SUN MADE IT A LITTLE WARM FOR A HIKE, BUT THERE WAS an occasional cool breeze that made the walk pleasant. Thomas had arranged for a bit of irrigation on the hilltop, to prevent him from having to lug water up the hill every day. It was a small concession, and he was pretty sure Somar wouldn't mind.

Somar, he thought, feeling the pang of grief again, as fresh as the first day. It had been nearly seven months since Somar had passed. He was buried here, on the same hill, just over the rise facing the colony. You could see the Citadel tower from that spot, and Thomas felt Somar would have appreciated that very much. He was there, always, watching the colony as it grew and thrived.

Somar's last act was to nominate Thomas for governor of the colony, and that had gone through with a unanimous vote.

First Colony. The naming had been unanimous as well. As Edward's people had arrived and mingled with the humans, interacting with those who had played host to them before they became part of the Current, lifelong friendships were made, strong bonds were forged. It was really a no-brainer to give the colony its name. The name it would have had, more than a hundred years ago.

Thomas had been overjoyed to see familiar faces appear from the lightrail, emerging from a relay that Alan had modified to be a sort of Current "port of call." He had been able to reunite with old friends. Seeing them, talking to them, Thomas felt a strange sort of relief. He had realized, at one point, that some part of him had believed that maybe he *was* responsible for the destruction of First Colony. He had believed all the press, it seemed, at least on a subconscious level. But here, on a new world, full of hope and opportunity, with all of those familiar faces talking and laughing and *living* again, it made the whole thing feel like a bad dream. The reality was here and now.

It helped that the Current could appear directly on the surface of First Colony now, without need of a shuttle. Alan's work was inspired by the technology they'd found on Taggart's moon, but the modifications and updates were his own genius. He was already yammering about modifying shuttles to enter the lightrail directly from the surface and Mitch was already threatening to brain him with a wrench.

Penny, on the other hand, was Alan's biggest supporter. It was her that had convinced him to travel, to see every colony world, and spend time on each of them. It helped that Edward could move them from world to world almost instantly.

Penny promised they would stay out of trouble, but judging by Alan's blissful expression and chronically mussed hair during every call, Thomas suspected trouble would happen eventually.

It was already happening for Mitch and Reilly. Without the distraction of things exploding around them, they'd had to find some other way to occupy their time. They had settled on the usual things that honeymooners settle on, and the result was that Reilly was due in about three months. Despite everything Dr. Michaels grumbled at her, she was still making shuttle runs, with Mitch glued to her side. Michaels chalked it up to "exercise" and let it go. Thomas allowed it only if they promised he'd get to be an honorary "uncle." Mitch told him he was a terrible negotiator — they were going to give him that anyway.

Taggart had given them some worry for a while. The ECF had been looking for scapegoats, and Taggart's ties to Earth First, plus the fact that he had built the kill switch on Taggart Prime, had made him a very tempting target. Somar had spoken at length with Admiral Norchek and some of the ECF leadership, explaining Taggart's role in resolving all of this, and saving the colonies from utter isolation. The Esool had pardoned him on all counts, and that had lent a great deal of weight to his defense. In the end, it was Alan who provided the defense that allowed the ECF to turn a blind eye. He presented the scans that showed before and after data of Taggart's brain. Louis and Taggart had merged fully, inseparably, and the result was that Taggart was literally not the man he used to be. The Taggart they knew may have been a criminal, but this man was innocent. At least, that was the verdict of the ECF.

Taggart and Alan had formed a strong bond as well. Alan's jaunt around the colonies was supported and paid for by Taggart Industries as part of Alan's new job responsibilities. But in truth, it was more of a gift, from father to son. Taggart could not stop talking about how proud he was of Alan, how brilliant the young man was, how he was going to change the universe for the better with everything he could create. He would be Taggart's heir in the business, Taggart had confided to Thomas. He was the son Taggart never would have had. He was Louis's son. It suited him.

Captain Alonzo had been ... *irritated* when he'd first merged with the Current. He'd spent quite a bit of time berating everyone about not interfering with the natural order of things, complaining that everyone was insubordinate to the point of countermanding his order to let him die. Over time, however, it became clear that he was exactly what the Current needed. He was a leader who could negotiate with the ECF on hard line issues, ensuring that there was a peace between them. It helped to have a strong alliance with the Esool. The entry of a third party into the treaty helped level the playing field, and the Esool now controlled their own lightrail technology again. The network was neutral territory. No one owned it outright. The Current could police that, ensure that it remained true.

And to keep the scales balanced, the Esool and the ECF each controlled kill switches for the lightrail. Failsafes abounded, and it would never again be as simple as flipping a switch. Taggart and Alan had worked out how the whole thing could be structured to prevent abuse. The Current agreed to terms of treaty and governance, regarding the lightrail.

In the end, it was all a very mutually beneficial relationship, as Alan and Taggart explored ways to improve lightrail travel using the Current as their model, and the Current gained access to the colony worlds as Alan's modified relays became standard.

Time would tell how stable the peace would be. There was fear across the colonies, and Thomas, of all people, knew that where there was fear there was the possibility of disaster. But that was nothing they could prepare for now. It was a future that *could* be. For the moment they had to focus on the present.

Thomas turned a spigot and heard the water rush through the line. The nozzles rose, and water sprayed in a mist, coating the sapling and saturating the ground around it. Thomas walked directly into the mist, unconcerned with getting soaked. He kind of liked it, actually.

He knelt in the grass near the sapling and took out his handheld, scanning. He smiled as he watched the display. Tiny arms, tiny legs. As the sapling grew, so did the small bud of Esool within it. Somar's legacy.

The "pregnancy" had been triggered by the blood bath, the treatment Thomas and Dr. Michaels had used to save Somar's life. They had been too late. The damage was too severe. At best they had given Somar a few months of extra time.

Admiral Norchek had explained that among the Esool, it was entirely possible for a male to produce offspring. In general, the females were responsible for this part of Esool procreation, but in the end any Esool could. The trauma to Somar's body had been severe, and the antibodies in his blood had done everything possible to heal him. When that failed, they preserved him the only way they could. They used his genetic material to create a whole new Esool.

Norchek visited this site often, usually with Thomas in tow. It had become known as Somar Hill, though no one was allowed to come here just yet. The area was restricted, by Governor's decree, until Somar's child was "born."

Norchek explained that the Esool could take more than a year to mature. It really depended on the conditions and the care they received. This birth would have its complications, of course. And there were some unknowns. This would be the first Esool to be born from an earthborn species of tree — a fact that Norchek encouraged Thomas to keep secret.

Apparently, secrets were just his thing.

It was fitting, that Somar's offspring would bridge the three races. An Esool, grafted into an oak tree from Earth, nurtured by the soil of the Current's home world. There was a poetry to all of that, and Thomas smiled every time he thought of it.

Alan had joked with him that he needed a new nickname. "You can't claim 'Destroyer of Worlds' anymore. Maybe 'Builder of Worlds' would be better?"

"Um, no," Thomas had said. "I think I'll stick to the one Norchek gave me."

"What's that?" Alan asked.

Thomas thought back to the last conversation he'd had with Norchek.

"The Esool are often born with a certain amount of genetic memory," Norchek had told him. *"The child will likely be born thinking of you as a friend."*

"I am his friend," Thomas said, *reaching out to brush the leaves of the tree.*

"More than that, I think," Norchek said. *"I believe you will make a better father than a friend."*

Thomas had smiled at Alan and said, "Builder of Worlds isn't much of a title, compared to 'dad.'"

A NOTE AT THE END

Afterword for the 2024 Edition

I didn't set out to write a trilogy.

I wasn't opposed to the idea. I mean, *Star Wars* was a big thing when I was a kid in the 80s, the era in which those first three films were the *only* three films. And later there were franchises like *The Matrix*. Again, another trilogy that's no longer a trilogy. Maybe I need to think about this.

I didn't quite have either of those two franchises in mind when I wrote *Citadel: First Colony*. I had other franchises on the brain. Television shows like *LOST* and *Battlestar Galactica* were pretty prevalent. But so was *Star Trek*, in its many iterations. That franchise, in particular, probably had the most influence on the way I wrote my ensemble cast, now that I consider it.

But here's the honest truth—the franchise that influenced these books the most wasn't a film or TV series. It was, much more appropriately, a series of books. Specifically, Orson Scott Card's *Ender* series.

That isn't a trilogy either. But for a very long while, it

kind of was. The first book, *Ender's Game*, was a seminal experience for me, back in 9th grade. I read that book after taking a standardize test, when I was trapped in a room for the next couple of hours with nothing to do. I have always been a fast test taker.

But that book, which I read cover to cover in just a couple of hours, changed *everything* for me. It was the book that made me finally notice, books can be *good*. Books can be *fun*. I must have more of these *books*.

I even paid homage to those books with the "molecular disruption disc guns." Named for the "Little Doctor," or "MD Device" from *Ender's Game*. Please don't sue me, Mr. Card. I meant it as a thank-you.

I had always been a writer, all the back to my first days holding a fat practice pencil as I learned to make letters on a page. But my stories were the same sorts of stories one reads, as one is coming up through the ranks of grade school. I was a huge fan of *Encyclopedia Brown* (another seminal series that had a big impact on my *Dan Kotler Archaeological Thrillers*). And of course I read Judy Blume and all who imitated her. I read the sort of books that tended to appear in on-campus book fairs. And those rare times I was taken to a public library, I tended to read some weird stuff for a kid. Books about psychic powers, Bigfoot, astral projection. Junior grade versions of headier stuff I would dive into later.

But *Ender's Game* awakened something in me. I suddenly needed *more* of this kind of storytelling. And I ended up reading everything I could find from Orson Scott Card. Which led to reading others in his circles.

Here's something I find interesting: Though I was a huge fan of the work of Orson Scott Card, it turned out I was not so much a fan of science fiction, as a genre.

I mean, yeah, I liked scifi. Spaceships, laser swords, aliens, all of it. Mostly as movies though. Or TV. The books didn't really appeal to me much. I can't quite explain why.

I was a huge fan of *Star Trek: The Next Generation*. I could tech-babble with the best of them. I tuned in every episode, even recorded episodes on audio cassette so I could listen to them on the hour-long drives to college. I daydreamed about being on the *Enterprise*.

But science fiction novels on the whole didn't really appeal to me. Not as much as one might think.

Instead, I gravitated toward stories that featured characters in a contemporary setting, that happened to involve incredible and fantastic elements. Books like Steven Gould's *Jumper* are a perfect example.

Come to think of it, I was also a big fan of Marvel Comics. Particularly *Spider-man*.

And now that I think about it even more, I always preferred stories with characters who were smart, often genius level, as well as having some kind of extraordinary ability or capability. And loners... I liked loners.

I'm starting to detect a pattern here. And a bit of *autorecognition*. Because most of my books involve characters just like that. Some even have superpowers.

Those books would definitely influence a book I wrote later, called *Evergreen*. As well as my fantasy trilogy, *Sawyer Jackson*. And the two leads of my two most prolific series, Dan Kotler and Alex Kayne (*Quake Runner: Alex Kayne*) were effectively low-key superheroes. Kotler is brilliant and has the ability to read body language to an eerie degree of accuracy. Kayne is a bad-ass who always thinks 20 steps ahead, and has a quantum-based AI she invented that can basically do anything.

Give them tights and put them in the *Avengers*, already.

Gotta tell ya... I'm learning so much about myself right now.

I have digressed, so let me loop back.

I didn't start out to write a trilogy. But for some reason, when I published *First Colony*, I finished that book by putting the words *Book One of Three* on the cover.

Why? No clue. But there it was. And I was stuck.

Writing the remaining two books became a point of pride and honor for me, but doing so was an exercise in high anxiety, dread, and drudgery.

Book One had come along easily enough. It was challenging, but it flowed. Book Two, not so much. It took a year of forcing, making myself get back to it in every odd hour I could spare. But Book Three? *This* book, that you now hold?

I think something like three years went by before I finally yanked this book kicking and screaming out of my brain.

It was hard, in other words. One of the hardest things I've ever done.

But here's a weird thing... when you do something that's hard, in this particular way, it changes you. It forces you to grow.

I came to a moment when I said to myself that if I really did want a writing career, if I really did want to be a novelist, then dammit, I had to actually *write*. If I didn't write Book Three, when would I ever write any other book?

So I sucked it up. I sat down and did some math. I figured out that if I aimed for a certain number of words for the book, and I committed to writing a set amount of words every day, I could knock out the first draft of the book in 30 days. One month of pushing myself, probably wanting to die the whole time, and I'd have it done and over with. And if I found that experience so horrible, I could bow out with at least the honor or knowing I'd *done it*.

So... I did it.

Thirty days, at a couple of thousand words per day. Every day. I'd get up at 4am and write for a couple of hours before leaving for my day job by six. And, if my brain didn't feel melty at the end of the day, I'd stop at a Starbucks and add to the count.

And, at the end of those thirty days, I had Book Three. *Children of Light* was a thing. It was real.

I did it.

And, as I said earlier, *doing it* changed me in fundamental ways.

Gone was my worry that I *couldn't* do it. I had the proof in my hands. I had the confidence that only comes when you pull it off, when you do the work, when you prove it to yourself.

And, I had a system now. A formula. I knew that writing a book was mostly a function of butt-in-seat, write-the-words, repeat.

So, I did it again. And then again. And again and again and again.

At this point in my career I have around 70 titles available, in multiple languages, worldwide. That's the kind of thing I used to sit around and daydream about, in my 20s and early 30s. And now, at a very young 51, I have that dream fulfilled.

In so many ways, *Citadel: Children of Light* is the book that actually launched my career. It showed me who I was, as a writer. It proved to me that I really could do this, and even better, that I really *wanted* to do this.

I hope you enjoyed this book, and the whole trilogy. I hope you go on to read more of my books, and that you really enjoy those, too. I hope you'll reach out to me and let me know.

And I hope you'll do the really hard, challenging, dreaded thing that you're putting off, so that you can also discover that *you can do it*, and that you *want* to do it.

I hope you go boldly in the direction of your own dreams.

J. Kevin Tumlinson
Liberty Hill, Texas
10 April 2024

BESTSELLING & AWARD-WINNING AUTHOR
J. KEVIN TUMLINSON

THE

COELHO
MEDALLION

A DAN KOTLER
ARCHAEOLOGICAL
THRILLER

"Kevin has crashed onto the action-thriller scene as only an action-thriller author can: with provocative plot lines, unforgettable characters, and enough adrenaline to keep you awake all night."

— —NICK THACKER, AUTHOR OF 'THE
ENIGMA STRAIN'

ABOUT THE AUTHOR

J. Kevin Tumlinson, award-winning and bestselling author of fast-paced, hopeful fiction and inspiring nonfiction. He and his wife Kara live in Texas, and she insists they travel the world to find new perspectives, new stories, and new tantalizing bits of history and thought to share with his readers.

Kevin grew up in Wild Peach, Texas, where he started learning the craft of storytelling at a young age. He began writing the moment he knew how, and never stopped. And, God willing, never will.

Kevin's love of history, archaeology, science, and philosophy has fueled every word of what he's written, and gives him all the excuse he needs to look closer at anything he finds interesting.

Connect with J. Kevin Tumlinson
jkevintumlinson.com
kevintumlinson.substack.com

ALSO BY J. KEVIN TUMLINSON

Dan Kotler

The Coelho Medallion

The Atlantis Riddle

The Devil's Interval

The Girl in the Mayan Tomb

The Antarctic Forgery

The Stepping Maze

The God Extinction

The Spanish Papers

The Hidden Persuaders

The Sleeper's War

The God Resurrection

The Demon Core

Dan Kotler Short Fiction

The Brass Hall - A Dan Kotler Story

The Jani Sigil - FREE short story from BookHip.com/DBXDHP

Dan Kotler Box Sets

The Book of Lost Things: Dan Kotler, Books 1-3

The Book of Betrayals: Dan Kotler, Books 4-6

The Book of Gods and Kings: Dan Kotler, Books 7-9

Quake Runner: Alex Kayne

Shaken

Triggered

Compromised

Aftershock

Historic Crimes Crossovers

The Man Below

The Outsiders Gambit

Evergreen

Evergreen: Book 1

Evergreen: Trace Contact

Citadel

Citadel: First Colony

Citadel: Paths in Darkness

Citadel: Children of Light

Citadel: The Value of War

Colony Girl: A Citadel Universe Story

Sawyer Jackson

Sawyer Jackson and the Long Land

Sawyer Jackson and the Shadow Strait

Sawyer Jackson and the White Room

Think Tank

Karner Blue

Zero Tolerance

Nomad

The Lucid — Co-authored with Nick Thacker

Episode 1

Episode 2

Episode 3

Shorts & Novellas

Getting Gone

Teresa's Monster

The Three Reasons to Avoid Being Punched in the Face

Tin Man

Two Blocks East

Edge

Zero

God Mode

Collections & Anthologies

Citadel: Omnibus

Uncanny Divide — With Nick Thacker & Will Flora

Light Years — The Complete Science Fiction Library

Dead of Winter: A Christmas Anthology — With Nick Thacker, Jim Heskett, David Berens, M.P. MacDougall, R.A. McGee, Dusty Sharp & Steven Moore

YA & Middle Grade

Secret of the Diamond Sword — An Alex Kotler Mystery

Wordslinger (Non-Fiction)

30-Day Author: Develop a Daily Writing Habit and Write Your Book In 30 Days (Or Less)

Watch for more at kevintumlinson.com/books